PULLING A TRAIN

(A VERY YOUNG)
HARLAN ELLISON®
AUTHOR OF "SEX GANG"
WRITING AS PAUL MERCHANT

An Edgeworks Abbey Offering

in association with

KICKS BOOKS
NEW YORK, NEW YORK

I

PULLING A TRAIN
A very young HARLAN ELLISON®
[Author of SEX GANG (Part One) writing as:
"Paul Merchant" and other noms de plume]

PULLING A TRAIN is an original Edgeworks Abbey® offering
in association with Kicks Books.
Published by arrangement with the Author
and The Kilimanjaro Corporation.

PULLING A TRAIN
by HARLAN ELLISON®

Harlan Ellison websites:
www.harlanellison.com and www.HarlanBooks.com

For more signed and personalized Harlan Ellison books:
c/o HERC: Post Office Box 55548, Sherman Oaks, California 91413

Published in 2012 by Kicks Books
PO Box 646 Cooper Station
New York NY 10276
Printed in the United States of America

Second Printing 2012
Hurricane Sandy Edition

ISBN: 978-0-9659777-5-3

Editor: Miriam Linna
Transcription and editorial asst.: Gigi Himmel
Design: Pat Broderick/Rotodesign
Front cover painting: Les Toil

www.kicksbooks.com

This one, if only he were here
to see it, and know how
much love and admiration
prompts it:

to the memory of
ROBERT CULP

Bobby. Demon. Glass Hand. Friend.

GARDYLOO!

Traditionally, usually, conventionally, this
position in the front matter of a book is site
for a list of the author's *other* books, major
titles, films, et al. To find such a chronology,
from #1 through about #90, for Ellison…
please hie thee to Pages 150-155. There is
only a finite amount of space in the known
universe. You may consider pp. 150-155
the variorum listing, and ever so accurate.

———————————————————

CONTENTS

Author Of Juvenile Delinquency Books Arrested In New York

NEW YORK (AP) — Police have arrested a writer on juvenile delinquency in whose Greenwich Village apartment they found weapons used by street gangs about which he writes.

Harlan Ellison, 26, author of novels entitled "Rumble" and "Deadly Streets," was arrested yesterday when narcotics detectives visited his apartment on a tip.

They found no narcotics but found brass knuckles, one pair studded with bits of metal to give a lacerative effect, a loaded revolver, a dagger and a switchblade knife.

Ellison said he had picked up the weapons while doing research for his books.

He was charged with violating the weapons law. "This," he said at a police station, "will give me material for my next book."

A WORD FROM THE PUBLISHER

BY MIRIAM LINNA

Harlan Ellison is the most effective genre-buster in captivity today. He barged into the literary world fifty-plus years ago by grabbing the flaming tail of juvenile delinquent fiction and dragging its bloody boots into the back room of the clubhouse for a switchblade hazing by a new breed of brassiere busting blue jean debutantes, hellbent for leather. He'd learned the JD stance during his service as war counselor in Red Hook's chain-swinging Barons, knew the real deal. It made Blackboard Jungle read like a gardening manual. The year was 1959. This was not the same old fluffernutter.

PULLING A TRAIN is our first collection of iconic early adult fiction by Harlan Ellison, written, as he likes to tell it, "for the buck," paying for room and board between sales to "real" magazines. The short stories herein have not seen print in generations. When they were in circulation, in assorted he-man publications back in the day, they bore mysterious by-lines like Cordwainer Bird, Ellis Hart, Jay Solo, Derry Tiger, Price Curtis, and Paul Merchant. For the collector quotient, *Lustful One* appears herein as the glorious *Nedra at ƒ:5.6* complete with potently pertinent mod age adlibs. These tales were hot. Brown paper wrapper hot. Hot enough to raise your hackles, and other things. They were street tough like the prime-cut JD shorts he was turning in to crime and mystery magazines during the same period, but crude and menacing beyond curative measures.

Ellison did to popular American fiction what Elvis Presley did to popular American music— he knocked it upside the head, so hard that the old gray matter was never ever quite the same again.

Out of print and off the radar for fifty years, these tales fairly levitate off the page with attitude to spare. Bad attitude.

Take it away, Cheech Beldone. Stag Preston awaits.

—Miriam Linna, editor
Bad Seed Magazine/Kicks Books
Brooklyn NY

INTRODUCTION

HARLAN ELLISON

INESCAPABLE CEMETERIES

If you pondered for a billion years, you could never appreciate how odd, how eerie, how un-settling it is for me to be writing an introduction to this first of two books never intended to see the light of day.

Doctors are lucky. *Their* fuckups get buried under headstones.

In literary circles there's an often-told legend. Don't know if it's true, or apocryphal, or just bullshit. But it goes like this: Ernest Heming-way, on the ship coming back from France, he having finished his *first* novel, before 1926's THE SUN ALSO RISES, was so disgusted and miser-able at what he had set down, that he tossed it over the rail, into the Atlantic Ocean, no trace or snippet of the manuscript of that novel remain-ing extant. We have only this legend. He buried what he considered a Frankensteinian misfit, and went on to glory.

I am Hemingway at the ship's railing, and my youthful indiscretions have risen from the deep, have ascended to print, and if you sat on a dune in the Gobi for a billion years, you could not know how discomfiting it is to be writing this introduction.

And so we halt our carriage of time fifty-two years later. Our carriage once known as SEX

GANG, now two volumes titled PULLING A TRAIN and GETTING IN THE WIND. I was twenty-five years old. Fresh out of two grueling years in the US Army, having been drafted after being thrown out of college, after having married—having married badly, but only half brain-dead aware of it at the time—and I was working as an editor for a men's magazine, the #2 slick men's mag in the game at that point. And on the side, I was not only writing day and night, and trying to unmire myself from the abattoir that had been my first youthful marriage, but I was creating, for a man I had come to despise, a man who casually battened on making people think he was all-powerful, I was creating a line of cheap mildly-titillating pseudo-erotic paperbacks. If you were reading in the Fifties, FOREVER AMBER had to be read under your bedcovers with a flashlight. LADY CHATTERLEY'S LOVER was being smuggled into the United States in the French-published Olympia Press paperback editions from Maurice Girodias in the way one smuggles true ivory horn today. William Burroughs was completely off the charts. So wore Alexander Trocchi (writing as "Frances Lengel"), Iris Owens (writing as "Harriet Daimler"), and Henry Miller. And FANNY HILL! Well, only depraved sado-masochists could get hold of an underground printing. School kids still read those little Tijuana Bibles, the eight page mini-comics featuring Joe Palooka with a dick the size of a schooner's mast, or Toots 'n' Casper in Porno Paree. And I created, lock stock and cover blurbs, a line of paperbacks for this odious person I came to loathe, a line called Nightstand Books; and they made him millions.

That's what I was doing at age twenty-five.

I was doing it for the buck. The guy I was working for was—in my constitutionally-protected opinion—a stone son of a bitch. I don't think he really liked writers, or trusted them: I think he conceived of writing as something other than "honest labor." But I made millions for him, so he put up with me. The mental anguish was just lagniappe.

The first time this book—now *two* books—was published, in 1959, as a slim, cheesy paperback collection, the name of the author was "Paul Merchant," the pseudonym I'd conceived to hide my perfidious activities. Originally, I wanted it to be "D.S. Merchant," the D.S. standing for "Dirty Smut." But the publisher got onto it and, somehow, "Paul" came into existence.

This time, the book is twice as long as the original, sort of like a freight train pulling a double load of flatcars and boxcars with the addition of more than a few stories from the same time-period that I think are pretty good. But then, what the hell do *I* know; I'm the yotz who wrote all of it. These are sort of new *old* stories. Pulling a loaded train.

But let me get to the title. I know you're dying to hear my twisted reasoning for putting such a bad taste politically-putrescent moniker on a modern paperback. Apart, that is, from just being an annoying guy.

When I was a kid, it was another kind of world, just at the end of the Great Depression, and there were thousands of younkers like me: On the road. Sleeping under railroad trestles, sharing gypsy coffee out of a tin can with "gentlemen of the road," hobos, and we called each other brother—or just 'bo. And when I'd manage to jump aboard an empty boxcar, it might be pulling a double, treble load. They were called clankers. But the phrase "pulling a train"—even though it started with riding the rails—came to mean something a lot less commonplace.

Hauling the freight, a double load, like SEX GANG, which is now a double-load of *two* books, got picked up by the street, and in the joint. Using it as a book title is merely a demonstration of my demented sense of what is black, dark, ugly humor. It is a tough title for what is supposed to be a book of tough stories written during a tough time.

"Pulling a train" is obscene.

When I first suggested putting it on this book, my wife told me she'd leave me. So I backed off fast, because I adore her, and I was going to call it, instead, DOING IT FOR THE BUCK.

Yeah, I know what the odious phrase means. It's old-time on-the-road syntax, outta the street and still being used in the slam by the lowest scum you can imagine. It's gangster slang from the 1920s, decades before "gangsta" was even conjured up by punks who are so stupid they think holding a .38 Police Positive sidewise is "cool." It came from a period when men treated women like "broads" or "gashes." I've heard hobos and cons and street thugs in packs use it since the 1940s. When it insanely came as a viable title for this book, my gorge became buoyant.

But I kept coming back to it.

Do not ask me why. Call it bad taste. Call it obsession. But PULLING A TRAIN of a double-load of stories is what it is, and I must admit, as

Monty Python put it, "It's a fair cop."

Sometimes in this life, there is no more truthful reply to Why Did You Do Such a Questionable Thing? than the helpless, "It seemed like a good idea at the time." That's what Napoleon said when someone asked him why he was ass enough to attack Russia in the killing winter. He shrugged, said, "I dunno; seemed like a good idea at the time."

These stories—which seemed, each one, like a good idea at the time—assayed across a lifetime of learning to do the job correctly, leaving some sort of decent literary footprint, seem to me now technically crude, written early on, written for the buck, to learn my craft on the job. I am a self-made man, thereby demonstrating the horrors of Unskilled Labor. I wanted to eat. So sue me.

Thus, I suppose my reason for the title is that they're the work of a tyro, and need not be enhanced by some extravagantly fatuous title. Old GI speak, biker phraseology, more than a touch gross. I reveal my roots. My wife, my Electric Baby honey, well, she let me have my way but she insists I should have my mouth washed out with a big bar of Fels-Naptha.

But since the destruction of the past and all its cues and clues has been effectively lost due to tv and the internet, most folks wouldn't even have figured out the reference, and only a handful, as weird as I, probably, will now "get it."

Considering the bulk of the shit that was nominated for Oscars and Golden Globes this year, hell, my title is as pristine as faerie dust.

Compared to what is "fit for consumption" these days, this book is baldly as it was intended: harmless. Back in 1959 it was lumped with "pornography," the devil's handmaiden, a vile tome guaranteed to blacken children's souls. Ten years later it was just silly pseudo- and updated-Victorian blue. No more infectious than THE PEARL. (Another obscure literary reference.)

Look, let's get something straight from the git-go. I got tossed out of college after a year and a half. I had the lowest average in the history of Ohio State University, at which institution one can only get such horrendous marks if one misses the game-winning pass. No student, I.

So this book comes to you with all its banners of youthful arrogance, inexperience, and indiscretion billowing in the breeze. It was written, piece by piece, by a smartass wannabe at the very beginning of what miraculously turned out to be a very long career. But when they were written, they were written fast, and by someone learning his trade. On-the-job training sounds noble, but often it's more mish-mosh than majesty.

No point in apologizing for the stupid errors and breaks in mature prose: They weren't written by a master craftsman, they were written by a kid trying to learn his trade, working for, well, the buck. *Just like all of you.*

...

So, there was this guy who wanted to get on *Playboy*'s gravy train, and he'd started a lesser imitation of *Playboy*. He needed to build an editorial staff. He thought of me. I took the job.

Went to Chicago. Actually, a suburb of Chicago.

Worked for him for a year, and around that time newsstands started selling what would now be called "soft-porn erotica," paperbacks with silly titles like SATAN'S SEX SLAVES and SIN WAS HER MIDDLE NAME and suchlike. Very, very tame crap, for its time...not to mention the present-day mode of Anything Goes. This was modern-day FANNY HILL sidewise "sex-stuff."

So this guy, of whom I speak, for whom I was working, asked me if I could cobble up a similar series of paperbacks.

Not only could I...I was better at it than those who preceded me.

If I recall correctly, this much later, the first of these (now referred to as) "sleaze" (or, sometimes "zilch") paperbacks were from imprimaturs such as Beacon Books, Bedside Books, Midwood, and on and on. Come to think of it, as long as I'm "being real" with you here, I think calling these books "sleaze" is a fucking insulting putdown word by plugged-up asshole academics and *NY Times* bestseller-list snobs feel way above their station. Fuck 'em, and the sleaze they rode in on, that's what *I* say, from my unassailable, literary nabob pinnacle, never forgetting my roots...as I wish they might remember theirs.

One-handed reading material, intended to keep truck drivers entertained in roadside toilets. In the trade we called them "stiffeners."

Today, they'd be laughed out of the room, so florid and so innocent were they. But at the time, oh, they were hot. Then: undercover; today: underwhelming.

And so I created, for a guy I hated, a line

called Nightstand Books. I devised plots, developed the formats, designed the cover art and sent everything off to the sadly overworked, underpaid slave-minions at the Scott Meredith Literary Agency in New York, who got a monthly fee for hiring brilliant (but overworked, underpaid) writers who, under their real names were writing some of the best trend-setting novels of their time. This was a fast fifteen hundred bucks for maybe a week's work. It was, as for me, lagniappe. It was for the buck. Creative minions. All of us. I did all the scut work, too: I made up the title, designed and wrote all the blurb copy, did the proofing and copyediting, and put out— to start—something like two or four a month. Went up to six a month very quickly. They took me about three days to put all four together, and they were written for a grand or a grand and a half by some of the best mystery and science fiction writers of the day…under pseudonyms.

They've published learned studies of that period, naming names. But I was the one who was the shadowy intelligence—misusing that word shamelessly—behind the bulk of what was selling hundreds of thousands of copies per month.

I made this guy I detested a couple million bucks.

Then I couldn't take it any more, and I got out just in time. (But that's another bit of history.)

He got me back by promising to give me my own "class" line of mainstream paperbacks to edit, and I came back from New York after a year to work on it, Regency Books, and to update Nightstand, for almost another year. Then I bolted again, and never returned.

At one point, early on in the first stint, we

needed a book fast, to fill a production hole, and I cobbled together ten reprints of my old hard-boiled crime-magazine and men's magazine stories (juvenile writing, at best), added a new title story, and it came out as Nightstand #1503. It was the third in the line.

"Paul Merchant" was a closely-held secret of mine for decades. I was damned close to ashamed of the book.

No point in even apologizing for those original eleven stories. I did 'em for the buck. I was married at the time, needed the money, and did what everybody does. I pulled the plow.

The stories are simplistic, not the greatest literature ever proffered, but I got a thousand dollars for the tome. That was big money in the Fifties. It was my third book published, in a lifetime of more than a hundred such. But the only one not under my name.

Many of the titles used on the stories had been changed outrageously by various editors, from their original manuscript titles (such as the Joycean *Portrait of the Artist as a Zilch Writer* to the goofy, but, well, less pretentious, *The Lady Had Zilch*) under the pseudonym "Cordwainer Bird." The less said about the appellations of these stories, the better.

For a very long time I didn't include this volume on the "book card" page of my more prestigious and better-known books. But Miriam kept at me, and now—as I mentioned earlier—I've somehow managed to live at least 77 years without winding up face-down under a railroad trestle, or with a bullet in my head.

I wrote a lot about street gangs way back then. I'd done an extraordinary amount of background work in the genre, up to and including actually running with such a gang in Brooklyn. So these stories are pretty accurate for the time.

But this is *another* time, a lot later; and I dunno, I'm not shamefaced about this work. It wasn't what I came to be known for, what earned me a lot of accolades and got me into the ENCYCLOPAEDIA BRITANNICA, holder of a science fiction Grand Master award, a couple of Mystery Writers of America "Edgar" trophies, Nebulas, Hugos, British Fantasy Awards, Honorary Degrees, and four "best of" plaques from the Hollywood Writers Guild...but it exists.

And I'm past the point where I need to hide my head for *anything*. I think the more you reveal, the less blackmailable you are. It ain't never the crime, it's always the cover-up that brings you down.

So Paul Merchant (and other *noms de plume* I used), who wrote for the buck and cops to it, rides again. Miriam, Susan, and Harlan Ellison are responsible parties. It is my hope that you won't think *too* badly of me, and might be entertained enough to try one of the other hundred or so books and movies with my name on them.

Caution: Please use both hands when perusing this volume.

HARLAN ELLISON
a/k/a "Paul Merchant"
31 October 2011

Sex Gang

(as by "Paul Merchant")

CHAPTER ONE
The Girl In The Alley

DEEK HADN'T WANTED TO RAPE THE GIRL.

It had been only a purse-snatch, initially. Scudball had come up with some good-cut pot, and Deek had been short of bread, so the quickest way to get some was a purse-snatch. But when he had reached out from the alley and wound his fingers in the girl's hair, it had become something else.

He had yanked her harshly into the black mouth of the alley, clapping his other hand across her full lips before she could scream. Then he had turned her... reaching for the handbag. But the girl had strangely begun to grind her hips against him, and Deek's passion had risen.

The girl pressed herself against him, more than his rough treatment demanded, and he felt the softly-rounded mounds of her breasts, the structure of her brassiere, the hard, raised points of her nipples, even through his T-shirt. His hand slipped from her mouth, but she didn't scream.

Instead, a soft, animal mewling passed between her lips, and she mouthed gently, *"Do it!"*

Deek's hand in the girl's hair flattened, cupping the back of her head. He pulled her mouth against his and her lips opened as the hot spear of his tongue entered moistly. He ground against her. The smack of her handbag hitting the wet cement of the alley was drowned out by the sound of her high heels as she moved her legs against his thighs.

Her arms went under his and palmed out against his back, her nails catching in the fabric of his T-shirt. They stood there almost silently, an occasional choking sob of passion coming from the girl. The faint glow of the street light was a constant reminder to Deek that he wasn't after fast sex but dough, and he moved slowly, steadily, the girl fastened to him. They went back down the alley, past the stacks of water-logged cardboard cartons, past the garbage cans, past the bricked-up doors. She hung on him, moving and moving and not even realizing he was taking her deeper into the darkness.

"Come on," she breathed moistly into his ear, "come *on!*"

She began slipping down his body, and he fell to his knees in front of her. "Right here," she urged him, guiding his hand under her skirt, "do it here."

Deek's hand touched the cool roundness of her upper thigh, and thoughts of the purse-snatch fled from his mind. The chick was really asking for it, and she didn't seem to give a damn how, when, why or where as long as it was NOW. He moved his hand up her leg, feeling the smooth skin indent under his questing fingers.

His hand met the rounded elastic edge of her panties, and paused only a moment touching the silken surface. He moved his hand again, quickly, sharply.

She gave a heavy, indrawn sob, and moved her legs against his.

Then she pulled him down on the cement of the alley, atop her. "What's the matter with you, what's the matter?" she begged.

Deek's free hand—without conscious volition—pressed the skirt up over the girl's thighs till it was bunched at her hips. She helped him roll down the panties, and aided him when he fumbled with himself.

Then, he rolled back on her, and again she moved, helping him, startling him by her brazenness. She directed him, urging his passion, and the fire burned suddenly between them... her gasp as he met her rang briefly in the alley and a leaping thought of the fuzz hearing at the call-box on the corner drew him away from her for an instant.

"Don't...stop..." she pleaded, grasping him by the hips, thrusting him down and in closer once more. The vagrant thought fled from Deek's mind and he plunged on, driving driving driving till she arched her hips from the cement, burying her teeth in his shoulder.

His hands went to her hips, and he lifted her slightly, their pistoning movements pinnacling higher and higher, till they chorused together, and her short, tearing wail signaled the decrescendo.

He lay there for a long moment after it was over, abruptly wondering what had happened... how had he come to lie in this alley when he had simply been after some dough to get a blast of pot...

The girl was still melted to him, her arms

tightly around his back and murmuring soft things, lost things that had no meaning, no reality.

He looked at her then, with the wet-shine of the alley reflected in her dark eyes, reflected like oil slick on asphalt. He saw the planes of her Italian face in sharp dark relief from the street light. He caught the nimbus of black hair that fanned out around her face, and the flaring nostrils. She was an attractive girl—a bit hard-looking, perhaps, but nice to see.

"What's your name?" she asked him.

She was looking at him, and he hadn't realized it.

Deek Cullen abruptly realized what he had allowed to happen to him. He had been suckered by a chick. On the move for a blast of pot he had made a pitch for her purse and been pulled in by her hot spread. Now there was a chick who knew what he looked like; a chick who was asking his name.

"Rumpelstiltskin," he said, pulling away from her. She started to sit up, the white pillars of her thighs bright in the reflected light, the skirt still a dark mass about her waist. He caught her across the mouth with a balled fist that knocked her back. Her head hit the cement with a whack, and she half-rose to meet his second blow. The fist took her under her left eye, and she gasped in agony.

Deek wound a hand in her hair, dragged the head forward and belted her three times crack! crack! crack! till her eyes rolled up in the sockets and she fainted.

Deek stood up shakily and zipped himself.

He wiped a hand across his mouth and ran a hand through his long, nearly-blond hair. He felt weak behind the knees, his shoulder where she had bitten him throbbed painfully and he had a drained feeling in his gut and groin.

He stumbled away from the twisted, unconscious form of the girl. It hadn't been rape, at least that much was in his favor. It had been as much her hunger as his. He stooped and grabbed up the handbag, ripping it open viciously.

He dumped its contents onto the cement and, kneeling, pawed through the rubble. Her wallet contained thirty-three dollars, a few subway tokens and perhaps another two dollars in change. He filled his pockets.

A pack of gum lay yellow against the cement. A nickel was a nickel. He shoved the gum into the right hand pocket of his jeans.

Then looking back at the muddy-dirty legs of the girl, and the darkness of her body where only shadows now penetrated, Deek Cullen slipped out of the alley, down the street...

And was gone.

The girl lay silently for the better part of an hour, then slowly, painfully, regained consciousness, regained all her thoughts, and one in particular: a face.

Deek Cullen lived alone in an eight-dollar-a-week room he shared with the cockroaches. His mother had been sent away when he was sixteen, two years before, for using a flatiron on Deek's father. Deek remembered the night he had come home with his mother from the movie and found the old man topping a broad from Herky's Bar.

It hadn't been so much that the old man was knocking off a piece, or even that it was in his own home, or even that the bimbo was a hooker from Herky's. But the cookie jar was empty. The old man had taken the vacuum cleaner money to pay the freight.

Deek's old lady had hauled the flatiron from the ironing board where she had left it when she had decided to take her son to a movie, and she used that thing like it was a battering-ram.

The hooker had gotten bloody from the spattering.

So they had sent Deek's mother away, and Deek had cut when the juvenile authorities came after him, and he had kept dodging for two years.

Now he was eighteen; a big eighteen, and sharp, and cool, and hungry, and devious. He could field a shank faster than anybody in the turf, he had more guts and brains than ninety per cent of the studs around, and he knew his way around. He knew how to use a rolled up copy of *Ladies Home Journal* as a lever to snap the door handle on a car he wanted to heist. He knew how to filter after-shave lotion and antifreeze down through a loaf of pumpernickel, making Sweet Lucy or Sneaky Pete to sell to the wet brains on the Bowery. He knew how to con the broads, how to duck the fuzz, how to tap a till, how to mug a lush, stiff-arm a mark and lead a rumble.

He knew it all; he was hard in the belly, fast in the legs and tight in the bed. Deek Cullen was a child of the gutters from which he had sprung, a creature of late evening and early morning, a deadly engine of destruction.

He belonged to no gang, because there was a cunning to him that decreed weakness in numbers. He was a shade under five feet nine inches tall, he had almost-blond hair that was naturally curly and that curled tighter when it got wet, he had steady brown eyes and a lantern jaw. The scars on his right cheek had come from a disagreement with an Armenian restaurant owner who had felt unkindly about being held up on Queer Street in the Village.

Deek Cullen had not been a virgin since the age of thirteen when a hot-box aunt from Racine had visited the family, found Deek sleeping in the raw while the family was working, and taken him like Hitler took Poland.

Deek liked his women, didn't drink, blew pot when he could afford it, did not attend school, occasionally worked driving a non-union soda pop wagon on the docks, bummed around, shot snooker, and in general wasted the time till something popped.

Deek Cullen should not have attacked the Italian girl in the alley that night.

It changed his life.

No one saw the girl looking through the front window of The Blue Parrot Billiard and Recreation Hall. Not even beady-eyed Blue Parrot himself, standing behind his cigar counter, endlessly tapping two half dollars against each other as he stacked and restacked them with the dexterous fingers of one hand.

Especially, she was not seen by Deek Cullen who leaned far over the table, making his unorthodox bridge of thumb and index finger, sighting down across the cue ball at the precariously-angled eighter.

The girl had an olive complexion, dark black hair, and a thin white band-aid under her eye where the faint discoloration of a black eye showed. Her mouth was bruised. She looked and she looked and then she smiled faintly, spitting on the sidewalk. Then her face disappeared from outside the pool hall, and the street was empty.

Two hours later, with an extra seventeen in dollars in the tight slit pocket of his jeans, Deek left Blue Parrot's emporium and headed up the street to the cafeteria.

The car was a canary yellow and black Impala convertible and it took the corner on three, hopping the curb as it roared on toward Deek. For a long moment his eyes were directed in their usual direction, gutterwards, but the sound of the panthers under the car's hood snapped his eyes up. He saw the grille and he saw the four eyes and he saw the two girls in the front seat...

The car sped up, two wheels on the curb, two in the street, and barreled down on him. For a second the bold horror of it paralyzed him, and then he felt a grip at the back of his T-shirt and he was yanked bodily off his feet, flung into a doorway, and lay there watching the car whip past.

The Impala jumped the curb, hit the street with a jouncing jar and careened off around the corner at the end of the block. In an instant it was gone.

Deek Cullen *felt* he had gone white.

He looked up to see a trim pair of ankles and two nylon-encased legs. They were good legs. Firm in the calves and tapered all the way. He followed the legs till they disappeared under a tweed skirt and then he followed the skirt till it blossomed twinly into a peasant blouse.

Her face was a pleasant face, but now strained with remembered terror.

Deek had difficulty forming his words. The breath had been knocked out of him, he felt shakey all over. "Th-thanks," he murmured.

The woman smiled vaguely and made as if to move.

"Hey, I said thanks," Deek started to rise. The woman stared at him oddly, and he saw a banked fire in her eyes that meant something... he didn't know quite what.

"That's all right," she answered. The voice was a controlled thing, almost aloof. There was a touch of New Hampshire in it. "I saw the car coming before you did. Those girls would have run you down. "

"Yeah," Deek said slowly, looking in the direction the car had gone. "Yeah, they would've. Thanks again." The woman was perhaps two inches shorter than Deek, and at least eight years older. There was a reserved beauty about her, and a small beauty mark by her lower lip heightened the delicate paleness of her face and throat.

"You, uh, you from the neighborhood here?" Deek asked. "Do I know you?"

The woman flushed slightly. "No, I don't think so. I'm the new social worker at the Settlement

House. On Kilgore Street."

Deek nodded absently. This was some dish. Good tight skirt across wide hips. Nice chest, the real thing, too. And she looked flustered. Good in bed but ashamed of it. Maybe even a virgin. Even at her age, well...maybe still cherry. Maybe.

"Well, I guess I got to show my thanks," Deek said suavely. "Can I buy ya a cuppa coffee?"

The woman flushed even more deeply. "No... n-no, I've got to get to the Settlement House. Perhaps we'll meet some other time." She started to walk away.

"Well, hey, thanks anyhow for savin' my life," Deek yelled after her. She nodded and continued walking. He took notice of the tight way her legs scissored in the binding of the skirt. "Listen, I'll, uh, I'll see ya soon, y'know?"

She didn't turn, so he followed her, suddenly limping. When she had grabbed him by the scruff of the neck and thrown him backward, his leg had struck the wall of the building. It took him half a block to catch her.

"Hey," he panted, drawing beside her, taking her forearm in his hand. "Y'don't have to run off like that, y'know. You saved a guy's life, the least you can do is stay and talk to him for a minute. That was quite a yank you gave me."

She had looked at him coolly at first, but now her full lips broke into a smile. "I was a counselor at a girl's camp," she explained. "Pulling kids out of the water built me up."

It sure did, Deek thought hungrily.

"I don't know my own strength, sometimes," she finished, smiling engagingly.

"You can strong-arm me, any day, doll," Deek said.

The words came out before he knew he was saying them. It was habit. It was the Great American Fencing Game, but this wasn't a ponytailed gang girl. This was a woman. She brought her hand back and slapped him full in the mouth. Deek's head jerked sidewise and he regained with a four-pronged red welt across his face. He grabbed both her biceps and yanked her in front of him.

"Listen, doll, nobody, but *no*body does that to me. You ever slap me again, sweetheart, I'll bust you up good." He shoved her away, and she stumbled back a step.

The look she gave him was half pity, half something else entirely. Then she spun on her heels, and walked away stiffly.

Deek stared after her till the image and anger had faded entirely.

Then he began to wonder—and worry—about the car with the two girls in it. He had recognized the dark-haired one with the band-aid on her face. It didn't look good.

They weren't old enough, either of them, to own a car like that. It had to be a heisted short. That didn't look good, either. They probably had studs for boyfriends who would lean on him if they found him.

Deek Cullen felt boxed in only slightly. And the pot hadn't been as good-cut as Scudball had indicated. It had turned into a bum trip all around.

That social worker…that broad with the fine body…

His mouth still stung where she had clipped him. But she was fine stuff to look at. Maybe soon, maybe one day real soon.

He decided on the instant to cool it for a while. No sense walking the turf when there was a kooky broad who wanted to run him down.

There wasn't any place to hole up, that was the problem. Sol With The Glasses had been sent to the Lexington farm—those stupid nabs thought they'd get the monkey off Sol With The Glasses' back if they spooked him for a while. They were wrong. That stud had no monk, it was an orangutan, that big, that bad it was.

Pinchy was shacked with a working broad who didn't like any of the coolsters around; she was grooming him for the strait jacket. The thought of Pinchy being hugged in wedlock was such a downer Deek had to smile. Old Pinch babe with his lech for little chicks like nine or ten. That working broad was going to have some nights that were real flakes. Poor Pinchy. Poor working broad.

That wasn't going to solve the problem, though. It had to be coolsville for a week at least. But where? How about Gary Teshlik? No, Gary's old man was still around and Deek didn't feel like a philosophy bout with the old guy. He had a thing about cats that didn't work steady. Road to ruin and all that jazz.

Abruptly, and odd that it hadn't come sooner, Deek knew immediately where he could duck out for a week.

Demoiselle's house.

And there was always the possibility of knocking off a little piece. After all, with thirteen girls in the building, and the smut campaign in town keeping the clientele to a minimum, there *had* to be a couple of the whores at least, who needed servicing.

Yeah, like nutty. Demoiselle's pad. Quicksville.

CHAPTER TWO
The Cat House

PATTY OPENED THE DOOR. She was dressed in a pair of tight toreadors and a white cashmere sweater. She gave Deek a strange look, as though to ask what he was doing there.

Deek shouldered past her and closed the door behind himself. "Where's Demoiselle?" he asked, mispronouncing it, warping it to "Demwazelll." Patty nodded toward the study. She shrugged her shoulders, as if unable to cope with the problem—with *any* problem—and hip-switched away.

Deek looked around the front hall of the house. It had been almost a year since he had worked for Demoiselle, doing odd jobs and acting as bouncer. But the old faceless brownstone still felt the same.

It was no secret in the neighborhood that this building was the biggest brothel in the city, but oddly enough, the payoffs to the cops lapped over onto the neighborhood; the cops watched out for the rest of the folks, too. So nobody said anything, nobody complained, the customers were quiet, the neighborhood a lot safer than others nearby. It was a reciprocating agreement between Demoiselle and the families surrounding the house.

Now Deek had returned to the house.

It still had that faint sex odor, like the warm, musky smell of a woman's body. He inhaled, and it brought back memories.

Then he knocked on the study door.

"Come on in, whoever," a mellow voice called through the oak paneling.

Deek opened the door and walked in. Demoiselle was at the secretary, writing in her check book. The woman kept her accounts religiously; it was a business to her, and she operated it with acumen and good taste.

Looking at Demoiselle was always an experience for Deek. He had never slept with her, yet every time he laid eyes on her, his hands went clammy with hunger. She was short, barely five feet tall, with raven-black hair that fell to her shoulders in smooth, perfumed waves. Her breasts were gigantic for a woman that size, but firm and upswept and well-formed. Rumor had it—though Demoiselle neither affirmed nor denied—she had been a streetwalker in London's Shepherd Market, and had married a GI who had ditched her once they arrived in America.

"Well, if it isn't the errand boy." Her smile was a sweet thing, a deadly thing: like a box of poisoned chocolates, and Deek's body ached with hurt for her. He could picture her small but exquisitely-formed body under him, writhing on the bed, on the floor, on the sofa...anywhere.

"What's new, Demoiselle?"

"A good question, boy. What do you want here?" She had a blunt way of avoiding questions she did not want to answer. Now she had put Deek completely on the defensive.

Deek wet his lips with his tongue. "I need a place to pad out for about a week?"

She shook her head. "No go, Deek. I can't afford to front no cops right now! It's all I can do, putting in the fix to keep the Assistant D.A. and those porn-campaign bastards off my tail. You'd be an extra handicap."

"It ain't the cops," Deek explained hurriedly. "I've got some, uh, gang kids lookin' for me. They been scourin' the turf. All I need is a pad for about a week; I'll work it off the same way I did last time."

Demoiselle's eyes, dark twins of caraway seeds, narrowed. "Last time, Deek? Do you remember why I fired you? You almost killed that Betty when you got to her that night. I don't want my girls bothered, Deek."

Deek Cullen smiled ruefully. "I'll be a real good boy, Demoiselle. I've grown up a lot since then."

She smiled, her thin lips bringing a dimple to sight in her left cheek. She appraised him boldly. "Yes, you have, Deek. Yes, you have. You've grown up quite a lot. You're closer to a man than a boy now." Her eyes swopt across the tight thighs of his jeans, examining every indentation and bulge of fabric. "Yes you have," she murmured.

Deek felt Christmas coming.

Demoiselle shoved back the chair and stood up. She continued to examine the character lines of his face, the way he carried himself. "All right, Deek. You can stay here for a while. But try to be a good boy."

The way she said it made Deek's face flame.

"I'm always a good boy."

"I know you'd *like* to be a good boy. I think you could be, too, Deek."

Deck Cullen looked at the woman carefully.

"There's only one thing I want. I want to be the biggest cat in the bunch. I want to be able to growl and watch 'em duck for cover. I want to be the biggest."

Demoiselle smiled indulgently. "Big hopes, Deek."

"I'm a big boy, like I said," he replied.

She smiled enigmatically. "Okay, Deek. You've made your point."

She went to the door and called into the hall. "Ginny, Ginny, come down here a minute." She turned back to Deek. "I've got six new girls in, Deek. They've been good here, they like the job, don't louse it up for me. I don't want any more Betty kind of business, do you understand?"

"Like I dig, take it easy. I'll be real best behavior, no sweat."

Then Ginny came through the door. She had the most magnificent breasts Deek had ever seen. They were like the rubber bumpers on a Cadillac. They came out at you and aimed over your head like a pair of 30 mm cannons, so you looked back over your shoulder to see at what they were aimed.

Ginny was taller than Deek, wearing high heels and an expensive Japanese kimono that was sheer enough to show Deek the hard, tight brown circles of the areolas surrounding Ginny's nipples. Deek's mouth felt flat and dry.

"Ginny, this is Deek. He's a friend. He'll be staying here for a while. I owe him a few favors, but you girls don't owe him a thing. So if he shoves, let me know. Until then, we'll accept him as a friend. You understand that, Deek?"

He nodded and smiled at Ginny.

She watched him through half-shrouded eyes.

Like a big sexy snake, Deek thought.

"Find him a place to sack out upstairs, will you, Ginny."

The girl patted her dark hair and shrugged. "Where should I put him? You want the marks to see him when they start coming in?"

Demoiselle extended her lower lip in a pout. "Put him next to you in the small bedroom. The maid won't be back for a week or so," she turned a smile on Deek, "until she dumps the monkey at Lexington Farm."

Ginny burst into a raucous laugh.

Demoiselle's scathing glance shattered the laughter into a billion ragged-edged remnants. Ginny moved toward the door. "Come on, kid."

Deek tossed a sloppy salute at Demoiselle and followed Ginny's well-packed bottom out of the room and up the stairs. He watched her legs form and lose form inside the kimono as she led him down the second floor hall.

The girl opened a door and stood aside to let Deek pass. "This is it, kid," she said, waving at the small room, its bed, bureau, chair and washstand. "Not much, but it's home." She started to move away.

"Hey," Deek stopped her, "why the big hurry. I thought maybe you and me could get acquainted." He laid a hand on her arm and pulled her up against himself, his other hand slipping inside the kimono, finding her breast. Ginny gasped at the abruptness of his movements.

She tried to shove him away, warning, "Demoiselle said we didn't have to take no crap from you, kid, so lay off."

Deek grinned hugely at her. He tried to pull her into the room but she freed one arm and swung her raking nails toward his face. Deek swung away and pinioned her arms to her sides, pressing her fleshy perfect breasts flat against his chest. "Now like take it easy, Ginny, and we can be buddies. I don't want no trouble, I just want to make friends…"

"You pay like anybody else, or you don't get in *me*, and that's the way it is, so…let…go!" Abruptly she brought up her knee. It caught Deek flush in the groin and he exploded with a sharp grunt of pain, falling up against the wall.

Ginny stepped back a pace, leveled her gaze, and swung a roundhouse slap that took Deek high on the mouth, spinning him and dumping him through the door of the room. He lay on his back and watched the silken paleness of Ginny's naked legs, in and out of the kimono as she walked away.

His crotch felt like someone had gone over it with a steam drill.

"I'll be seeing you a little later," he promised her retreating back. In a whisper.

That night, Deek began earning his keep.

In a city where organized vice was a commonplace item, the "small businessman," such as Demoiselle, had twofold problems: the righteous, good citizens and their committees, campaigns and cops…and the Syndicate. Unionize the cribs was an old idea, and the Syndicate had done it many years before, but occasionally circumstances allowed a scrupulously clever entrepreneur such as Demoiselle to keep operating.

But the pressure to come into the main organization was there. It was there, and that first night, Deek found out just how much pressure there could be.

The marks started showing a little after seven-thirty.

The first one was a short, fat, bald man who looked like a miniature Edgar Kennedy. He eyed the girls wetly and settled on a petite brunette with good legs and small hips. There wasn't even time to con him into a byplay with a drink or dancing before he had her by the wrist and up the stairs. Demoiselle frowned, but said nothing.

Then two buyers for a lingerie department in a Denver department store made the scene and were a bit more gracious. Ginny and a tall, statuesque, redhead, who shaved more than her legs to hide the fact that she wasn't a natural redhead, took the buyer.

After a while all fifteen of the girls were busy, and even Demoiselle had picked a John for a quickie, business was so good. There was a silent, but standing, order to "move 'em out" after they'd had their jollies, to allow the SRO crowd bed-space.

Only once was Deek called on to quell a disturbance. A truckdriver type, intent on proving his masculinity, had tried to use a garrison belt on one of the girls and when Deek burst into the bedroom (none of the doors had locks on them) the weapon had been poised to fall on the naked girl.

Deek had grabbed the belt as it swung back, and whipped the lantern-jawed trucker with it. One solid swipe with the leather glove filled with half dollars and the trucker was in a haulable condition. Deek had dumped him in the first passing taxi—after carefully removing only what Demoiselle had said was due—and told the cabbie Far Rockaway. Where in Far Rockaway? Any goddamn where in Far Rockaway, stupid. Here's a twenty.

That had been the only incident.

Until the Syndicate arrived.

There was no warning. They came through the back door facing the alley, and they came right through into the front rooms without so much as a by-your-leave. But there were several split skulls as they passed customers in the halls. There were six of them, all packing Police Positives or .45s with silencers, and they came on like the Hole In The Wall gang.

Demoiselle had packed her John off by that time, and was sitting cutting up a few touches with several SRO clients in the front room, when the hoods broke through.

Deek had been lounging in a corner of the big, overstuffed sofa, eating a nectarine from the kitchen. But, wiping drool off his chin, he left the living room to dump the pit and wash the stickum off his hands. As he started to kick open the swinging door between living room and kitchen, he heard a thick commanding voice:

"Stick tight, whoor, an' nobody gets whacked."

Deek edged against the wall and nudged the door a fraction with his palm. He was rewarded by a slit of light from the living room, cut off by the doorjamb, that included Demoiselle's bare

knee, part of the sofa, the pant leg of a custom-
er, and the barrel of a sturdy .38 Police Special,
aimed about a foot and a half above the silken
knee.

Deek let the door slide back. Oh Jeezus! Some
cooling pad! Here he was in the midst of some
kind of a Syndicate action; he had long known
Demoiselle was faking it out, trying to spook
the Outfit either into leaving her alone or giving
her a bigger cut on the proceeds, but he hadn't
dreamed it would go sour while he was cooling
it here.

All the same, he had to do something. Bad.
Very bad. *But it looks like I'm the only one that
they haven't got the drop on yet. They don't know
I'm here. So cool it. So cool it out the back way.*

It appealed. It appealed real good.

But it was chickening, and Deek couldn't
make that scene, even though he knew it would
be smarter if he did. He looked hungrily at the
kitchen door that opened onto the air shaft and
the basement windows across the shaft…the
basement and the street beyond. From the living room he heard the vicious pop of a silencer
and the crash of something heavy hitting a coffee table on its way to the floor. So the big boys
had waited long enough, had bided their time
long enough, and now weren't bothering to ar-
gue. He heard another pop and a shrill, short
scream.

Deek bit the back of his hand. He had to do
some God damn thing! *Some*thing! But what
could he do? He looked around the kitchen,
at the white enamel table, the big refrigerator,
the sideboard and the mounted knife-rack, the

huge containers of coffee Demoiselle always kept filled for the marks...

The boiling coffee...

The knives...

Deek grabbed a pot holder from the sideboard and removed one of the big dripolaters from the stove. He gripped it till it was so tight his hand went white. At least twelve, fifteen cups there. Plenty of hot, blinding stuff. He drew a serrated-edge bread knife from the rack and palmed it underhand, knife-fight-style, away from his body.

Then he slid to the door, raised a foot, and kicked like a sonofabitch! The swinging door was hit with all he had in him.

The door whanged open and slammed against the wall of the living room before starting back on its return trip. The three gunmen who had come into the living room—leaving their three companions elsewhere to clean up trouble—turned on the door and fired almost simultaneously. Deek leaped through without really thinking, and dodged to the side like a broken-field runner.

With one convulsive movement he hurled the open container of scalding coffee at the two gunmen nearest him. The container flashed burning black liquid completely over the two and their shrieks of agony cut through like banshee wails. Deek dove forward and slid under the coffee table, the knife he held slashing up to shield his face.

He drove the blade into the lower thigh of the third gunman, and ripped down.

He felt bone and cartilage give, and the gunman fell with a wild, whimpering mewl. There was blood all over everything. Deek wrenched the blade out of the man's leg and rose up over his victim, straight-arming the bread knife down once, twice and again, chest, neck, and neck for the killing blow. Then he had the man's .45 and he found it a simple matter to pump four slugs across the room into the two blinded Syndicate men who stood scraping at their scarred and blistered faces.

The living room was a debacle.

Demoiselle was dead, lying across the sofa, her skirt hiked over her thighs, a bullet hole between her eyes like a dark, deadly period, as black as the finishing stroke it had been.

The mark was dead, too, crumpled beside the broken coffee table matching the one Deek had dived under. The other mark was nowhere in the room. Deek was trembling so badly he thought he might vomit. He had already soiled his underwear.

There were more in the house. He was sure of that. But it didn't matter now. He didn't owe any allegiance here now that Demoiselle was dead. All the good turns that had been done were wiped away now. The slate was clean. She was dead, and he wasn't about to buck the Syndicate for Auld Lang Syne.

A gunman came through from the hall with Ginny, naked and wrapped in his grip as a protecting shield. She was half-conscious with terror, and there were finger marks across her huge breasts where the gunman had taken his time with her before the irregularity of the gunshots from the living room had brought him forth. He had expected something wrong, but not the scene that greeted his eyes. One companion ripped to shreds, pumping wetly onto the rug, and the other two dead, thrown in a corner like bags of dirty garbage.

The pop of Deek's silencer startled the gunman and only the moist redness that ran down over his face—where his right eye had been—convinced him that he had been shot. Ginny had been a poor shield. The gunman scrabbled at his shattered face and screeched like a goosed showgirl. Then a simon-stupid expression split what was left of his face and he died...standing there. He was leaning against Ginny, and she was too petrified to step out of the way.

Deek clambered up from the floor, sweat rippling his vision. The girl was pasty-white from face to fanny. "Come on, moron," Deek mumbled, grabbing her by the shoulder. As he jerked her toward himself, the body of the slain Syndicate man toppled forward, broke its nose as it crashed against the sharp edge of the undamaged coffee table, and sprawled onto the rug.

"There's two more of them...they...th-they're up there k-killin' everybo—"

Deek cut her off with a disinterested shrug. "That's *their* look-to, not mine. The ones left haven't seen my kisser, Ginny, and I ain't about to let 'em, either. I'm splitting. C'mon."

She was a drag at the end of his arm. "C'mon, willya, fer Chrissakes!"

"I can't," she moaned. "They're up there killing everybody and—"

"*Forget it*, willya!" he snarled. She looked again at the massed corpses in the living room, and her eyes took on a deathly-green cast. She stared at Deek as though he were something inhuman, some sort of public executioner. "I'm—I'm n-naked," she objected.

"Tell it to the Legion of Decency," he brushed away her remark. "Lady, there's a couple of hoods up there who'd as soon kill me as spit on me...so rumble your tail or I'll leave you here for them to shoot."

She whined again, and he dragged her into the kitchen, through the door and across the airshaft, carefully having closed the door behind them. Then into the basement where he found a pair of too-big overalls and a filthy T-shirt which she donned, trembling.

In a few moments they were out on the next block, and walking fast. Instead of cooling down, things were getting hotter by the moment. Deek Cullen was becoming scared. Worse than scared: trapped.

CHAPTER THREE
Bowery Passion

IT WAS A BOWERY LOFT. Deek had known the cat who had lived there until the building had been condemned, and though most of the front of the pad had gone when the wreckers had sent their half-ton smashing ball through the wall, it was dark and warm and best of all, private.

Ginny sat slumped against the wall, smoking. The bright orange tip of her butt winking harder then softer as she dragged deeply. It was that kind of night. When the sky bit off in little flakey chunks and what you thought meant a helluva lot. It was that kind of night, and Deek was feeling tired, even watching the girl.

Sometimes it all seemed so damned useless. He was an I've-been-around-too-much-maybe eighteen years old, and what he wanted was something so big and so hungry sometimes he felt it wasn't worth the trouble. Just lie down and pull the dirt over and get cool, very very cool. Like sleep.

"I'm cold," she said from across the room.

"Eat crap," he murmured back at her. Not because he meant it, or because he was angry, but because he felt very much out of it, very hung up on being hung up, and she was a big-teat nothing with no brains and no moxie and nothing but her sense between her legs. So he said it.

"I'm cold…"

He leaped to his feet. "You're no more goddam cold than I am, you stupid slut, so shut your big mouth or I'll dump you out through that wall. Now go the hell to sleep." He sank back against the empty wall, and scanned the night sky through the rent in the masonry.

It was a flake, the whole damn scene. A lousy flake.

Forget all the jazz that came before. Forget all the stinkhole years in the railroad flats and the smell of sour liquor from somebody else. Forget all that. Take it just from the chick in the alley and the two of them in the car and that broad from the Settlement House, and the rumble in Demoiselle's pad. (That made his stomach heave up, all the blood, and the sight of Demoiselle's thigh…knowing it was going cold, all that death, Jeezus!) Just take it that far. And how did he get there?

Why me, he kept thinking, *why me*? And the answer came, as clear as a waterfall into a pool, *Because you stink*.

That was it. The cosmic someone who gibbered and capered and set tho scales the way he pleased, that transuranic imbecile with the constipated intellect, *he* had decided Deek Cullen was going to have a rough row to hoe, so Deek Cullen was pulling tricks from his ears but suddenly, just to stay alive.

Oh, God, it was piling up again.

It was starting all over again.

The running. The loneliness. The hungering for hundreds of intangibles. Not the things he could feel and touch and see but the blasted, hurting intangibles that gnawed gut-wise and never left him alone. That was what could kill you. Outright. Walking down the street and clutching the temples because there was hurt here, hurt and terror and no escaping.

The girl said something from across the room, and he cursed her viciously. Death to the infidels! Philistines all!

Deek Cullen lay back, laid his head back against the cool soon-to-be-demolished wall, and wept very quietly. Partially because it was release from the terrible tension and terror of the night—a night in which he had killed four men without hardly knowing he was doing it—and partially because he was what he was. And it wasn't enough. Not for him. Not for anyone.

He felt something soft on his cheek and looked up. The girl had left her position across the room and come to him on silent feet. She leaned over him, her long, dark hair falling over her face and caressing his cheek.

"What's the matter?" she asked politely; there was concern in her tone.

Deek turned away. Nobody should see a man crying. "NOTHING!" he shouted at the wall. "Not a damn thing, so scram. Lemme alone."

"You poor kid," Ginny said, slipping down beside him. He could feel the heat of her through her overalls. The clothing smelled rank from the basement where he had stolen them.

"Don't give me that goddam *kid* routine," he drew back a hand to belt her. "I'm eighteen. I'm eighteen with the biggest—oh, hell, get away from me …" He turned back to the wall once again.

Ginny leaned over him again and her hand went to his ear. "Cut it," Deek said, as she played with his ear, running her finger around the inside shell, tickling him. But his voice wasn't convincing.

Abruptly, he wrenched away from the wall and grabbed her by her dark mat of hair, pulling her face down and crushing his mouth against hers. Her lips parted and his tongue entered, searching. She growled—a small animal—and slid down into his lap. His tongue searched her mouth, every warm crevice, every hidden recess, a small counterpart of larger desires. His hands slid under her hair, locked at the base of her skull, flattened out around her ears. Her eyes opened momentarily, then slid shut dreamily as he nipped at her lip. Suddenly he drove his tongue to the roof of her mouth and she thrust her hands reflexively down between his legs.

Deek jumped as though speared with a live wire, and rolled her off his lap onto the dirty floor. He lay beside her for a moment, then slowly withdrew his hand and ran it down her neck till he had it locked in the fabric of the T-shirt. He felt the neck band of it tight against her throat, held there by the tautness of her encumbered breasts. With a vicious jerk he ripped the flimsy covering from her. Her breasts exposed, she lay there on her back returning his kisses, and now guiding his hand onto her massive breasts. As he touched her warm flesh it felt as if he might burst into flame! The nipple stood up rigidly with her animal passion. He ran his finger around the hard, almost square-topped protuberance, feeling small puckers of goose flesh rise with each touch. He continued massaging the breast, making wider and wider circles with his talented, frenzied hand, but always returning to the nipple to stir her more deeply. Ginny was going insane with hunger for him.

Her hands came up his back and clawed through cloth into flesh. He could feel her raking him, but it only heightened his passion. The overalls were large on her and he tried rolling them down off her hips, but even though she arched up to allow him freedom, they would not pass her hips. He unzipped them and slid them down off her long legs in one fluid movement. He sat back on his haunches for a long moment staring at her naked body, one knee bent up, offering delicious shadows in the dark triangle of her thighs. He laid his hands flat on her legs and slid them up between, coming down on her as he did so. His hands were quick and then moist and, once, she even gasped as he penetrated her. Then he worked, stirring her with all the innate deviousness of an untrained youth. Soon she was rising off the floor, her back and belly covered with sweat, clutching him, pleading for his final torture.

She helped him off with his pants, and when he lay on her again she did not wait for his own time, but grasped him and delivered him to the seat of warmth and they thrashed terribly and higher and higher till she arched up off the filthy floor completely, carrying him with her, and buried her teeth in his shoulder, to stifle the shriek.

Then they fell back, and Deek worked a few minutes longer till he, too, was wracked by an apex of sensation.

It was like the jack-hammer biting out bits of a street, gnashing at the heated air with all the frenzy of machinery tormented by humans who didn't know how far it would go before running amok.

He plunged down once again, heavier, just to go as far as he could, and gripped her by the buttocks, pressing in and her in and himself in and then it was over, as quickly as the crushing of a dusty moth.

Done.

He withdrew and rolled off her. She gasped at the brutality of the loss of inner warmth, pulsing. "You don't have ta'—"

"Shuddup," he murmured, and found his pants with his hands in the darkness. When he was dressed he snaked a cigarette free of the crumpled pack in his pants pocket, and lit one. The girl was a pale smear against the many-hued darkness of the corner.

"You're a real strange character," she said, softly. He drew in his belly with momentary annoyance, then caught himself before he sliced her with words.

Why was he bugged?

This girl had only done him favors. So why be annoyed at her? No reason. But all the reasons of all the people who—like this girl—had done their part to screw up his life. Moms and Dad and the fuzz and the two girls in the car, and Demoiselle who had known he couldn't resist the broads and had hired him for a whorehouse... all of them. All of the dirty little people with a touch of rot about them who feasted on the sight of a good kid with a little off-direction getting shafted in life.

He could not understand the thoughts that ran through him. But he knew he was unhappy, and dirty, and lonely and worst of all... and had he known enough to say it, God help him... damned.

It was a long night, and he smoked enough to yellow the inside of his middle and index fingers. When morning came streaking the Eastern sky, like fingers of murky urine in a dirty grey pool, he felt worse than before. His eyes were grainy and his skin felt moistly clammy.

The girl lay where she had been taken, her naked belly staring roundly up at him, and the curling dark mass of her womanhood beckoning.

Deek ground out the last cigarette under his heel and decided to split that scene before he got hooked on it, hooked on her, like the needle-noses down on Junkie Row. He found his way down the rickety, bombed-out stairs, and hit the street wishing he had a ticket to Anywhere.

He counted the change in his pockets, and it added up to a pair of greasy eggs on toast at The Hammer.

He made his way along the Bowery, back toward the Village and a little anonymity.

The Hammer was a diner, run by a Puerto Rican with bad breath, who had been thrown out of the Army because he could only understand (he said) two gringo phrases: "Chow down!" and "Line up for pay!" The food was bad, but the price was right. Deek ate his eggs without looking at them; it was enough to have to down the swill without seeing all the yellow-grey blotches of old bacon fat dried on the slimy hemispherical surfaces of the eggs.

Once more street-borne, he stared at the thinning charcoal horizon line of buildings against the sky. New York was a good place, for all of it. For all the taint and all the angry, all the need and the hungry...it was still the best

of all. Still the one scene that could be spooked
without cutting a guy down to stupid talk and
crab grass. Even New Rochelle, so near to the
Apple, or the Bronx, or even the square end of
Brooklyn with the tract houses butt-into-butt
on one another—they were the sort of scene
that wigged a guy.

But New York…

He took the IRT back to the turf. Someone was after him, for sure: no question; but
dogged or not, it was all he knew, and with the
shank in his dresser drawer, and with trusties
around to help out in a tough bind, it was the
one place to settle.

He cursed himself for having dodged out. He
knew he should have stayed close and dug the
scene with the chicks in that car. But he'd run
scared. Now he was back.

He came up out of the subway kiosk and
caught the early morning sun straight in the
eyes. Brown eyes that were good eyes, and eyes
that fronted a brain with something perking. It
was his scene. A tough one, because it had to be
a tough one because it was a tough one and like
that. But it was his, all his, and he was the loner
that walked through it.

While the kikes banded in the Long Knifes
and the Puertos ran together as The Blooded
Imperials and the Eye-talians stuck together as
the Little Hands, he walked among them solo.
It was a rough go, but he was tall, tall man in a
world of little men, and he had picked up scars
to prove he could do it alone.

(The child who saw Deek Cullen leave the subway kiosk was ten years old with small specks of

snot clinging to his under-nose. He wore U.S. Keds and a pair of jeans that were spotted with yellow paint. His hair was uncut, unkempt and unclean. His name was Cockroach in the turf, and he had been talked to by a girl without a name who had said, "If you see Deek Cullen, you come tell me and it's worth half a buck." At 8¢ a Popsicle, half a buck meant hours of cool mouth and sweet insides. The child named Cockroach saw Deek Cullen leave the subway kiosk, and he ran down one of the side streets with a number for a name...ran down the street to find a girl to tell he had seen Deek Cullen. Come out of a subway station kiosk and gimme my half buck.)

Deek Cullen struck off across the street of cobblestones—left from another Manhattan era—and made for his pad. It had been all kinds of water under the dam since he had last seen that pad, and Deek Cullen, who had killed *maybe* in a rumble, now knew he had killed for real.

And he liked the idea.

He liked the feel of the thing, though not the sight of it. But he had done it, and from now on, he was something new. It was another Deek Cullen who came back from the runaway.

His room was so small if they had screwed handles on it, they could have buried him in it. The room consisted of a brass bedstead that sounded like the Anvil Chorus when he had a broad in it, a dresser with drawers that stuck, a sink permanently encrusted with black scud around its inner surface, and a heavy cardboard wardrobe that held the meager store of his clothing. A threadbare throw rug covered a miniscule area of the bare floorboards.

It was cheap to live there.

It served the purpose.

Who needs the Taj Mahal when it's a drag to live at all?

Deek Cullen slipped off his shoes without unlacing them, and considered going down the hall to the bathroom. The mental image of the water closet convinced him he didn't need to go right now. First a little sleep.

Beyond the tiny room the sounds of the loft building melted familiar. It was an old building, with once grand apartments cut up by an immigrant landlord into moneymaking smaller wall-holes. It was early morning; just after everyone had cut for work who had to cut for work, and the old ladies who lived off the pension checks still out doing whatever it was old pensioned ladies did in the early day. He could tell he was next to alone in the building. It had that feel.

Abruptly he realized that he wanted the knife, and wanted it badly. He slid off the bed and went to the dresser. Under a pair of heavy wool gym socks he found the Italian stiletto and took it back to the rack with him.

He laid down and looked at the closed knife for a long time. At the mottled white plastic that banded the knife on two sides. At the gleaming white of the steel edge closed into its trough. At the little button that hung in so cleverly waiting to be pressed. At the intricacy of the lock at the back of the blade.

Then he held it up and away from his body, with his hand lengthwise down the closed edge of the body-form, and let his thumb settle idly, lightly, just caressing the button.

Then a press...

Then *snick*! and it came up swift as a cougar striking. The sunlight muggily streaming through the dirty lone window caught the blade and flashed its presence on the colorless wall in a bright smear of reflection. Deek felt more secure, more at ease. It had been foolish to ever go off and leave the knife, but when you're scared...

He heard footsteps in the corridor.

His face came around on the pillow, his ear turned toward the door, and his mouth grew tight. It wasn't likely anyone would be walking the hall of the building at this hour, unless it was someone who didn't belong there. All the stiffs and old ladies were off and about their business at this hour.

He started to sit up in the bed, when the knock came, twice, rapidly. Deek slid his legs off the bed, and stared at the closed door.

Whoever was on the other side, it wasn't someone he wanted to see. He had been away, and now he was back, and already someone was knocking. Which meant either the knockers had been coming at regular intervals to check him— which was bad—or the knocker had known he was back in the turf—which was worse.

Should he answer?

His tongue balled up in his mouth, and he decided to keep quiet, let the knocker decide no one was home, and go away. He laid back down on the bed, keeping the knife very close.

Outside, he heard the rustling of feet. More of them. He heard a soft whisper of undertalk, and as he began to rise on one elbow, to consider the problem again. A blow struck the door that made it cave like a bow inward, sending splinters ricocheting across the room.

"Hey!" he yelped, thinking only of the cost of the door when the landlord saw it.

Another, fiercer, smash was leveled against the flimsy partition, and the door shattered off its ancient lock and flew inward, crashing against the wall.

Deek leaped from the bed, the knife away from his side, his body coiled for the strike.

When he saw the ugly muzzle of the zip gun, he stopped. He stepped back again, and finally hit the wall. The blood drained from his face as though he had been told he was dead.

He was hung up but good this time. There was no fire escape from the room, the one window hung three stories above the sidewalk, and the door was blocked off. There was nothing to hide behind, nothing to throw, and the knife would certainly be useless against that zip, held so professionally in the hands of the girl in the doorway.

She had a band-aid under her eye.

It was the girl Deek had attacked and beaten in the alley. And she wasn't alone. She had friends. Three of them.

The first girl was a beast. Perhaps one hundred and eighty pounds, swathed in a grey sweat shirt and jeans, on her feet a pair of stomping brogans. The knocker who had smashed open the door.

The second was a weasel. She was five feet tall at the outside, more likely four foot eleven, and looked like the classic study of rickets in youth. Her eyes were small and red and watery, and her nose was the same. She looked furtive, and her lank blond hair hung to her shoulders with a sickly resignation, as though it had no place else to go.

The third one was unbelievable. She had hair as black as a pound of coal dust. Her eyes were black, too, and strange with olive and gold glints. Her skin was very pale, and her breasts were the most magnificent things Deek had ever seen. They were high and large, and strained against the front of the sweater the black-haired girl wore.

But it was the girl in the front, holding the zip gun, that Deek stared at. He stared because the gun stared back at him.

"C'mon," the beautiful one with the ebony hair commanded. "We're goin' to meet some people."

Deek brought the switch blade into sight.

"Drop it or Pootzie blows a hole in you," the girl said. "Drop it and let's go."

Deek stared tightly for a moment, then dropped the knife. They moved aside to let him pass out of the room.

CHAPTER FOUR
The Gang Bang

THEY HAD THEIR CLUB ROOM in the basement of an abandoned factory. It was set back from the street behind a cadaverous grey fence, and the property was neither condemned, nor up for sale, nor even of interest to a buyer. It was dead-hold property the owners might have liked to completely forget, using it as a tax dodge.

The girls had made a base there, and they led Deek through a rent in the fence; he could see that there was a very definite organization here. The leader was obviously the girl with the cruel black eyes, and the other three her side girls. The one with the zip, Pootzie, kept staring at Deek the way she had stared that night in the alley...almost hungrily. It made Deek feel dirty, exposed.

There was a sloping door, set into a ground dormer, and the six foot fullback with the sweatshirt and jeans lifted it with no difficulty. Her face was a poor sculpture cut from the fleshy equivalent of granite. She was the ugliest girl Deek had ever seen; as ugly as the girl with the black eyes was gorgeous.

"Inside," the black-eyed one said, shoving Deek.

He stepped down into the ground dormer, and there was a stairwell. It was dark below, and he gripped the rough stones of the wall with his fingertips. Behind him the four girls followed, and the fullback, last, closed the dormer door down atop them once more.

Deek downstepped till he felt a concrete floor. Then he stepped aside quickly, in the darkness, and felt the passage of Pootzie beside him. He reached out, twined his hand in her hair, dragging her toward him, and slammed her as hard as he could across the breasts.

She dropped the zip gun, and Deek went scrabbling for it, his ears filled with the sound of Pootzie crying from the pain. He felt the wooden stock of the home-made weapon, and was about to lift it when the fullback came down on him like a Panzer unit.

Her fists locked together, she raised her arms and brought them down into Deek's face like a jackhammer; Deek tumbled forward, the pain all-consuming.

When light filtered back into his world, he was stretched out on a rug that smelled from cat urine and potato chips. He looked up, and saw more than the girl's legs. Her skirted body hung nearly directly over him, and he had an unobstructed clear view of full, white thighs, perfectly curved legs and pink pants.

He didn't move, and after a moment the girl stepped back. It was the one with the black eyes. "You think you got away with it, din'tcha, guy?" the girl said. There was a hardness even in her voice that surprised Deek. So beautiful, and yet with an inherent cruelty to the form of her full lips, the color of her eyes, the way she inclined her head to speak.

He didn't answer.

"Somebody messes around with a Cat, he's lookin' for trouble, and when somebody *beats up* a Cat, he better hide! You didn't hide so good, buster. So now we get our rocks by evening the score."

Deek watched as the girl went to a cabinet in the wall. It was made of old orange crates, and—he suddenly realized—seeing the room in one flash of observation—most of the furniture was the same.

The girl took down a belt, a thick garrison belt, and Deek could tell from the way the edges of the buckle shone in the light of a beaded floor lamp that had been turned on, that the buckle was honed razor-sharp.

"Terri, take off his shirt," the black-eyed girl commanded. The fullback moved away from the wall and bent over Deek. She lifted him under the arm with one hand, getting him into a sitting position, and wound a meaty hand in the fabric of his T-shirt. Then she ripped. It came away in two big strips, across the front and back, leaving the sleeves still clinging ridiculously to his biceps.

Pootzie moaned at the sight of Deek's bare chest.

He glanced at her, and it drew an accompanying glance from the black-eyed girl. "Yeah, that's our problem with Pootzie," the girl with the belt interjected. "She's always got a hot rash. Can't stay away from the guys. You picked a good one to try and mug. You're lucky she didn't tear you apart with that hot squat of hers!"

Deek stared at the hungry eyes of Pootzie. The girl still held the Italian attractiveness of the night in the alley, but now that he knew she was a nymphomaniac, he could detect the harsh lines of unnatural thirsts around her mouth and eyes.

"I didn't jump *her*," Deek said defensively, "she jumped *me*!"

The girl smiled nastily. "You know me?" she asked. Deek shook his head. He had never seen the girl before. "My name's Fabia. Fabia DeLuca. That mean anything to you?"

Suddenly, it did. It was a name he had heard around the turf lately. The girl who had the new club. The Cats, yeah that was them. A bunch of real stud chicks, who didn't give a damn, and weren't attached as Deb auxiliary to any male gang. They were just out on their own hook, run by this Fabia DeLuca swinger.

There had been plenty of rumble all through the turf about them. Swiping hub caps, robbing candy stores, and doing it better than the guys who'd been at it for years. But even more, they were making the big sounds all around the territory because of the way they mugged lushes, picked up sailors and hoisted their kicks, managed to avoid the nabs, and in general had a ball, without any guys around.

Deek Cullen looked at the dark-eyed girl with more respect. And more fear.

"What'd' ya want with me?" he asked. "Why'd ya try to run me down in your car the other day?" He knew the answers, but it kept her from using the honed buckle on his face.

"Wasn't my car," she said. "We heisted that short to get you. And don't play stupe. You better know right now, stud man, we don't take to any man mussing up one of our girls...even Pootzie. Cause once it happens, we become bait, and I've got too much business to worry about my girls getting involved fighting off men."

Deek grinned up at her.

"What the hell's so friggin' funny," she demanded, coming at him with the belt.

"You. The way you look at me and hand me that crap about men. You're just a lousy lay is all, or you got something screwed up in your plumbing. That's the only reason you're such a mean bitch." There was a laugh from the direction of the little weasely-looking girl. Fabia De-Luca turned on the smaller girl.

Hatred blazed nakedly in her face. "Listen, Thumb, shut your friggin' mouth or I'll cut you to pieces!" The little girl, now identified as Thumb, said nothing, but there was a sly sparkle in her beady eyes.

Fabia turned back to Deek. "So that's your big analysis for today, is it? Well, we're gonna have a little demonstration, tiger, just to see how good *you* are. Pootzie!"

Pootzie came to Fabia's side, and the naked lust in her face was difficult for Deek to take. "You ever been in a gang bang on some chick?" Fabia asked Deek.

It was rhetorical. He wasn't expected to answer.

"Well, you're gonna see a gang bang on a *guy* this time...and guess who the guest of honor's gonna be?"

She nudged Pootzie. "Strip," she commanded her.

Pootzie began to strip off her sweater. She stood there for a moment in bra and skirt, then bent over to unhook the bra. Her breasts hung only slightly, and she seemed almost bathed in sweat as she stared at Deek's naked chest.

"Hey, listen, what're ya, out of your mind?" he objected. Terri, the fullback, lifted him under the arms, and without seeming effort threw him onto a dirty sofa against one wall of the club room.

"Take off your pants," Fabia said sharply. He sat there, numbly, half intrigued by the idea, and half repulsed. A female monster, a sick-looking sneaky little broad, a nympho and a chick so good looking it hurt in his groin…what a menagerie. "Go on, take 'em off, or I'll have Terri *pull* 'em off you."

He unzipped his fly and tried to slide the pants down off his legs. They caught on his shoes and he had to remove them first. Pootzie stood swaying, her hands going involuntarily to her breasts, crushing them, twisting the nipples, in a frenzy of mounting passion. "Come on, come on, come on," she kept murmuring, her lower body within the skirt swaying so nervously the fabric billowed out like a parasol.

Deek lay on the sofa, clad only in underpants.

"Okay, Pootzie," Fabia tagged it, "he's yours."

It was as if a signal had been given.

Pootzie ripped at the zipper at the side of her skirt, and when it stuck from her ferocity, she ripped at the material, peeling the rags down off her hips. She kicked the skirt away and Deek saw she was wearing a two-way stretch. For a moment. Then it, too, was in a corner. She wore no underpants. The girl stared hungrily at Deek's nearly naked body, and her hands came out like twin grippers.

She took a stumbling step, almost feeble with anxiety, and fell atop him. Deek tried to ward her off, but in a moment she had ripped the underwear from him, and was gazing hungrily at his body.

He felt like something about to be devoured.

Her hands were hot as they touched him, and a stream of fire shot up his legs. She lay down on him and ground her body closer, closer, till he thought he would lose his senses.

The other three girls watched, their faces weird mixtures of pleasure, lust and hatred.

Pootzie's hands kneaded and probed, and when she thrust her face down at Deek's, his hand came up to grab her neck. He kissed her furiously, then, not caring that the others were watching, not caring that they might kill him, not caring about anything but this girl and the fire that burned between them. He slipped his body tighter to hers, and she opened her legs slightly.

Her breasts flattened out against his chest and he could feel the hard, sharp, hot points of the nipples pressed into his flesh like heated raisins into dough.

The girl was gibbering mournfully in some animal-born tongue, pleading for pain, pleading for penetration and the final joy.

But Deek was relishing this. He had an audience, and the conception of heating four birds with one stone, so to speak, amused him.

She was thrashing now, demanding him with her hands and with her body. But he wasn't ready. He rolled her against the sofa, and laid atop her, placing his face into the valley between her large breasts. He took one hard, fiery nipple into his mouth and she shrieked with

intermingled pain and pleasure. Then…then…
he took her…

It was wild and untutored, and at the moment
of ecstasy she slammed both hands against his
back so hard the breath left him and he col-
lapsed on top of her, not having been satisfied.

She rolled out from under him, and Deek lay
there gasping, still sweating, and wondering if
he was going mad. This was something from de
Sade, not a modern city.

"My turn," said Terri.

He looked up, ashen. The huge girl was standing in nothing but her gym shoes, her great,
pendulous breasts trembling like suet. Her face
seemed to be a Rushmore carving, hanging
there in limbo above him. He felt a constriction
in his belly as the huge girl settled down beside
him on the sofa. Her breasts were as large as his
head, and he could see even the fine blue veins
at the areolas.

"C'mon, hot shot," she said, bending down
to him with her dark brown hair falling over in
great waves, "let's see how you do with me."

Then her mouth was crushed to his, and she
met the barrier of his lips and parted it as though
it had never been present. Her tongue snapped
against his teeth and involuntarily he opened his
mouth to receive the hot dart of moisture. She
kissed him with all the power and ferocity of a
great animal, and Deek felt himself rising once
more to the female invitation. He reached up with
his free hand—one was imprisoned by the heavy
mass of her breasts—and dragged her head back
by the hair. He rolled out from under and in a moment was astride the great bulk of the girl.

Her body was already lathered, and waiting to receive him. There was an instant of sharp report, when he took her brutally, and a spasm of her mewling, "Oh oh uh, yes, that's it, that's it, oh you, oh *youuu*, YES!" and she lay like a spent balloon of gas. Large and wasted and satiated.

Deek climbed off the sofa, his legs almost giving way. Terri lay puffing and flushed on her back, her hands thrust down into the cavern between her legs, raised like church steeples against further violation. On the rug Pootzie still panted at the memory of her passion, and wetted her lips constantly with her tongue tip.

Deek's head was feverish, and he saw things inside his eyes that made no sense. Yet he managed to challenge, "Okay, there's still two of you. Which one now... huh, which one?"

He was praying neither would say anything, appalled at the erotic spectacle, but the little one, Thumb, made a sound from her corner and said, "My turn, now it's me. He's got to take me..."

He saw her out of the corner of his eye as she came toward him. A small girl, almost pathetically bony, and he was repulsed. She was not ugly, though there was such an air of weasely conniving about her that it distorted what might otherwise have been attractive features.

The girl lifted her skirt and showed her thin legs.

"I can't do it the way Terri does it," she said, "but I know tricks." She came on, the skirt gripped firmly in her hands, her pathetic chest urged forward.

"No, not you," Deek said.

Fabia DeLuca answered from behind him, "I've got the zip, stud. You'll play our little Thumb's games, or I'll pop a hole in you they'll be able to march the Chicago Rams through."

He turned and saw she meant it, holding the firing pin of the zip gun back, ready to drive the .32 slug through the car radio antenna barrel. "Okay," he agreed. He moved to the sofa.

Terri still lay with her eyes shut, and he grabbed her by one arm, yanking her completely off the sofa as he would haul a bag of meal.

Thumb lay down without removing her clothes, but with her skirt bunched up around her hips. Deek lay down beside her on the big sofa, and her eyes seemed to glaze over with a milky white film. She began to writhe against him, her hands going to him. At first he lay flaccid in her attentions, but soon his fever began once more to rise and he took her.

Then, abruptly, Deek floundered and fired and it was over for him, though she continued, till it hurt him. "Stop it, stop it, damn you!" he ordered her, trying to drag her mouth off himself. But she was like a turtle that will not let free till thunder crashes.

Deek lifted a fist and smashed it against the side of her head, sending her tumbling from the sofa. She lay on the floor, and cried at him, "Hit me! Hit me again! Please, beat the hell out of me!"

Though so weary he felt he must drop in a moment, Deek Cullen arched back his foot and kicked Thumb in the mouth. Full on the lips he caught her, sending her spinning, her face bloody. She cried with unrestrained joy. It was passion for her, more than anything else. He straddled her body and lifted her from the floor by her hair.

His palm came out and cracked across her face. Then back. Then again and again and again, till she begged him for more, and worse, and he doubled his fist, driving it into her stomach. She writhed against the blow, and fell toward him, blessing him, damning him, loving him.

Deek was repulsed by her, and insane with the fury of what he was doing. He could not see reason, had no idea what havoc he was wreaking on the girl's face and body, till finally, in a final fit of brutal torment, he laid both hands locked-together, and brought them around in such a roundhouse blow that it lifted her from the floor and dumped her at his feet, unconscious.

Deek Cullen stood back, his body a torrent of sweat. Around him in the room the three women lay spent in their own particular hells of passion.

Pootzie, satisfied by the driving urgency of his sex. Terri, obviously sex-starved and anguished for a man, empty and satiated on the floor where he had thrown her. And Thumb, beaten senseless, ecstasy upon ecstasy from the rain of his fists on her body.

Only Fabia was left. Fabia DeLuca who now stared at him, the zip gun held tensed in her hands.

"I don't know how good I'll be, but it's your time now, Satch." His words were hollow with fatigue. He felt he might lie down and sleep for a month. Yet she was staring at him in mixed wonder and—something else.

"The first time," she said, and the zip gun lowered a trifle. "The first goddam time a guy has been able to take it. They usually tear 'em apart. You're good bait, daddy, you're somethin' else. I think we might get together real good."

Yellow lights flashed on and off in Deek Cullen's head. The zip gun lowered a trifle more. It was aimed at the floor now. He walked toward her. This was a woman. The others, they had been bodies, sick inside, one way or another. But this was a woman with a full, lush, ready body, and if there was anything left in him, Deek would have her.

The zip gun dropped to the floor as he met her in the center of the room. His hand crept between their bodies and instinctively cupped her breast. She gasped, and her great dark eyes closed.

There was no room on the floor, so they made love on the sofa, and she was better, much better than all three of the others combined. Her body was a live flame, and her lips found his almost magnetically.

Once and twice, and almost three times, till Deek Cullen fell into a slumber of spent passion that included a dream. Of a girl with ebony hair and a hungry mouth.

Good dreams, but crimson.

CHAPTER FIVE
A Dose of Terror

IT HAD BEEN VERY EASY. Joining the Cats was a cinch after a demonstration such as he had given. They were a strong bunch...ruthless... unyielding...self-sufficient...but they needed their sex from time to time, and it was better for them to have a man they trusted, one who could service them all, one who could run with them, as one of them.

Deek liked the idea. He had always been alone, always avoided joining up with a bunch of studs, because they sapped his strength with their own weaknesses, but the Cats were different. They were a hungry bunch, and they were like him—taking what they wanted from anyone that happened to get in their way.

It was enough for Deek. He had killed and now he was with a group that could also kill.

They went out on their first job the next night. It was a warm, maybe too warm, summer evening, and Deek took Fabia by the arm as though they were high school kids out for an evening walk to the movie. The other three followed a block behind them.

Fabia and Deek turned into the Park.

The other three took the other entrance, and came at him—right angle. Deek and Fabia walked arm in arm, talking softly, the perfect picture of young love.

A picture that seemed to be mirrored by other couples in the dusky verdancy. They walked on, penetrating deeper among the hushed couples necking on the grass or leaning against the boles of trees, till finally Fabia nudged him in the side.

One couple, well-dressed and lost in each other's smiles, were walking down a side trail, further and further from the park lights that cast such feeble circles of light. "Let's go," she said, and urged him on faster.

"Where are the girls?" Deek asked, casting about in the gloom for their shapes. He could see nothing. There was no sound of snapping twigs or crunching leaves from beside the trail.

"They're where they're supposed to be," she answered tightly. The boy and girl ahead of them had paused and stepped slightly off the path, to share an embrace. "Now!" Fabia snarled in Deek's ear.

They moved in on the couple, and Fabia went for the girl like a panther. She dragged her bodily from her lover's grasp, and threw her to the ground. Deek came up beside the boy, startling him as he watched his girl beaten by Fabia. Deek grabbed, whipped the kid around by the collar. Fabia was methodically beating the girl senseless, and now stooping to remove her watch, purse, earrings and bracelet, as Deek's fist chopped solidly into the boy's belly.

The boy doubled slightly, and though he tried to swing in a killing uppercut to finish the job, Deek missed as the boy turned slightly with the punch. It grazed off his neck instead of solidly connecting, and did more to shudder Deek's arm than incapacitate the boy.

Then Deek's opponent did a peculiar thing. He sidestepped, reached out and grasped Deek's wrist. Deek was more amused than alarmed, for he mistakenly assumed the boy was hanging on for support. He was even more surprised when the boy, obviously schooled in judo, whipped Deek across the hip, and threw him with a crash into the bushes.

Deek fell heavily, rolling twice and coming up groggy.

The boy was trying to peel Fabia from the body of his girlfriend, when the Cats came out of the woods. Terri carried a white glove, loaded with half dollars. She brought it up and back and down in one fluid movement that carried the home-made blackjack to its target with all the punch of a howitzer. The boy caught it across the skull, just above and behind his right ear, and he staggered as though pole-axed.

Terri spun him with her hand, and whipped the coin-filled glove, a deadly blackjack, side-wise. It took the boy across the eye, and he fell without a sound, his face shattered from eye-brow to the bridge of his nose.

Deek dragged himself from the bushes, and stood trembling from the force of his fall. "Je-ezus," he murmured at the fullback, "you took your goddam good time about getting here."

Terri grinned her orangutan grin. "We usu-ally handle it ourselves. We don't usually have a big strong guy to help us." Thumb snickered obscenely.

Deek said nothing, but he was burned; wise broads. He bent to the task of stripping the guy. There was a watch, a class ring, a wallet with sixty-two dollars in it, and a fountain pen. He also took the belt and tie. That was another five dollars saved.

They passed the haul to the girls, who disappeared with it into the woods, and they continued walking…looking for another strike.

If the looted couple awoke and found Deek or Fabia, they could prove nothing, for the evidence had gone with one of the girls, while the other two followed along in the darkness off the trails. That way they could make four strikes a night, sending the evidence off with each of the three Cats, and finally taking their last haul themselves.

It went off well. It was a foolproof plan. They soon grew to be experts at it.

A craftsman in any trade soon draws attention, too.

She came to him in his room, and there was concern on her face. "I heard you were the boy they were after, at the Settlement House," she said. "They haven't made a definite identification, but I knew it was you. I'd like to help."

She still had the beauty mark above her lip, just the same as the day she saved him from Fabia and Pootzie in the assassinating car. The broad from the Kilgore Street Settlement House.

"Help me? I ain't done nothing."

"They say you and some girl are behind all the muggings in the Park."

"Who's *they*?"

"The police. They came down to check our records. They have half a dozen suspects. You're one of them."

"They got the wrong stud. So do you. Beat it,

I wanna sleep."

"I helped you once, perhaps I could do it again."

"Hey, like you don't hear too good, do you? I mean like cut out, willya, kiddo. I gotta get some sleep."

She sat down on the edge of the bed, and looked at him carefully. "Listen to me Deek. I can help you. I can get them to give you a suspended sentence, if you'll turn yourself in, and tell who the girls in the gang are?"

Deek leaned up on one elbow, and was very close to the sweet smell of her, clean and soap and some unnamed perfume that made his head swim. "I tell you, you don't know who the hell you're buggin'. I ain't done *nothin'*!"

She stared at him levelly, and he remembered the fire he had seen smoldering subtly in her eyes, that day in the street. Now she was here, was it only because she thought he was in trouble, and she could help? Or was there something more, something more darkly primal Deek could recognize, something he could understand only in his genetic awakening?

He reached up, and traced the line of her high cheekbone with one finger, and felt her stiffen at his touch. So it *was* something else.

His hand came down onto her shoulder and gently, almost reverently, he bent her toward him. Her eyes began to close as she neared him, and then, as though she had been waiting for her face to reach that point in space since she had come into this room, they slid to slivers and closed entirely, and she gave him her mouth hungrily.

He pulled her down, rolling atop her, grinding down between her legs with his hot body. His hand locked with hers, and he spread her arms symbolically, pressing tighter to her, and finding her tongue with his own.

He probed the moist wetness of her mouth, stirring her to small sounds, and then pulled away, burying his face in the sweet-smell of her hair. He worked his mouth down and found her ear. It was always a gamble, but when it worked, it saved time.

She responded. The warmth of his breath and the hot spear of his tongue at her ear stirred her more than even his kisses, and her torso writhed under him.

"Uh, uh, oh, there, *there*, that's it, that's where it is, do it there…" she murmured.

Then his hands slipped down and grasped her skirt. She arched up off the bed so he could slip it over her hips, and her panties came down equally as swiftly. Her tender lower areas were revealed, and he used his hands to drive her into a frenzy of passion.

"Take me…you filthy bastard…you OH! you good, so good, solo goood…" she was raving and rolling her hips back and forth as he took her.

She was good, because she had been pent up, and he had released her.

When it was over, she lay there with her eyes closed. After a while she arranged her clothing as though she had done something shameful. And when she left, it was more with shame than sorrow. There was an unspoken something in her manner that bothered Deek.

The woman—he suddenly realized he had never known her name—might just be rocky enough to give him trouble.

The trouble came later that day. He was walking down the hall from the bathroom when he saw them. Two of them, and they had fuzz written all over them. "Hey! You!" the one with the wart on his cheek yelled.

Deek bolted. He spun on his heel, dropping the towel he had used to dry his hands, and ran back down the corridor, to the window facing the fire escape.

He didn't wait to open it, but shattered it with one booted foot. Then he was out on the fire escape, and hesitating only for an instant.

Animal cunning told him he had time enough to get out of the cop's sight, and he climbed *up* the fire escape, rather than down. They would automatically assume he had raced down and lost himself in the alley. They would spend their time searching the streets for him, while he used the secret pathways of the rooftops.

In a moment he was on the roof, across it, and leaping through space to the building adjacent.

It took him only a matter of minutes to move five blocks away, down through another tenement, out onto the street, into the subway, and away.

He knew he must get to Fabia and the Cats.

They would be planning another job, and it was getting on toward evening... they might move out at any moment. He must stop them. If they got caught, they'd rat on him, and he had to protect himself.

He found the factory deserted, and waited in

the cool dimness of the basement for the girls to return. Thumb was the first to make the scene. She came down the steps and lit up greedily when she saw him alone.

"C'mon, honey Deek," she invited, pulling her skirt up to expose her legs. She wore no underpants. Deek looked away in disgust.

"What's the matter, I ain't good enough for ya now?" she snarled, and dropped her skirt back over her legs.

"The fuzz are lookin' for us," he said. "I don't know how far behind me they are. I gotta get outta town. Fabia's got the dough stashed away. I want my share. I need it to blow this town. Things are too hot for me. I want to split the scene."

Fabia's voice spoke from the stairway: "What's the matter? You turning chickie on us, Deek?"

He stood up and walked toward her. "The nabs. They came to my pad. The broad from the Settlement House must of told them I was the guy who'se been pulling off these Park capers. They came after me. I had to cut. I want my share of the bundle, and I'm splitting this town."

"We aren't ready to break up the partnership, yet, Deek."

"Screw that noise. I said I want out, and out is where I'm goin'. Now either you give me my share or I take the whole boodle."

Fabia smiled nastily. "Find it."

Deek reached up, she stood two steps above him, and grasped the neck of her dress. He gave a tug, and she came tumbling down to him, her breasts flattening against his chest. The knife was in his free hand. He let it come up into view slowly, and then pressed the button.

It clicked open, and she stared at it with her black eyes, a tingle of fear in her veins. "Now listen, you filthy whore. You take me to that dough, or I'll cut you to pieces."

He meant it, and she was suddenly terrified.

Thumb said something dim and threatening behind Deek, and he felt a rush of air as she came toward him. He spun, still clutching Fabia's dress, and lowered the point of the long Italian stiletto, like a lance. Thumb had a broken bottle they had used as a lamp, and she was coming for Deek's face. The knife took her just below the neck, in the hollow where her collarbone broke. It went clear through, and she spouted like a geyser as she went down, gurgling; the white, dead centers of her eyes rolling out of sight.

Deek wanted to vomit. It was horrible. But he had to tough it out. He was in it now, all screwed up, and he had to beat it out of town, and fast.

"Now. You gonna take me, or do I feed you some of that like the punk?"

Fabia's face was so white, her black hair had a domino contrast to it. She nodded dumbly. She would take him to the cache.

They left the basement, and she moved off before him…the stained knife still extended in his hand. He followed her down the back streets and through the alleys, till they came to the junkyard where the great wrecking machines stood empty sentinel duty for no one.

Fabia moved down the line until she had come to one of the wreckers with a giant mag-

net hanging dead still in the air above them.
"I buried it there," she said, indicating a spot
among the rubble.

Deek broke the knife, closed it and shoved
it into his jacket pocket, and fell to his knees,
digging. He scrambled among the bits and pieces of broken and smashed metal, the old beer
cans, the debris, trying to find the black metal
box they had seen Fabia put the money into.
For safekeeping, she had said. And when we get
enough, we cut out and find a new turf, or have
ourselves a ball somewhere, or maybe even go
down to Mexico for a few weeks. It had been a
good idea, then. But not now.

Deek was spreading the hole, throwing rubble and dirt back like a dog on the dig for a
bone. He scrabbled frantically, and almost did
not hear the clatter of the gears shifting.

But he did hear, and the machine was rusty
from disuse, and he was able to leap up and
away as the great magnet dropped with a hiss
and a roar, ratcheting down its chain.

It struck the earth directly where he had
been, and sank to half its own depth in the
ground. He looked up into the cab of the machine, and Fabia DeLuca looked back down on
him with a hunted, frenzied expression distort-
ing her features.

"I'll kill you for that!" he screamed, coming
after her.

She leaped out the other side of the machine,
and sprinted agilely across the junkyard. Deek
whipped the knife free from his pocket, snicked
it open and took off after her. She was like a rab-
bit, seeming to find paths through which she

could wiggle, without looking for them.

Deek had difficulty negotiating the twisted stacks of scrap metal, lumber, lathe and old auto bodies. In a few moments she had disappeared through a break in the fence surrounding the junkyard, and Deek Cullen stood alone.

He cursed her violently. He had to find her. He had to get the money. He had to get out of town before the nabs were onto him.

Where would she go?

There could only be one place. Back to that damned factory. It had to be there, because she had no home, and it was probably where she had *really* hidden the boodle. He picked his way out of the junkyard and stuck back for the factory. When he got there, it looked deserted.

Yet he could not take a chance. He crept around to one of the first floor windows and pulled himself up to the widely-protruding ledge. It wasn't difficult to force the old and rotted lock open, and he slipped inside, into the empty building proper. There had to be an entrance leading to the basement rooms. He could surprise her, come down on her from above, and beat the hell out of her till she told where the money was.

Then he could shank her, and cut before anyone ever knew she was dead. It'd be years before anyone checked that basement. He had it made.

The door to the basement was in the rear of the massive tool room area, and he opened it as stealthily as possible. It squeaked once, and he gritted his teeth in fury.

There was no stairway, but rather a concrete ramp that spiraled down to a furnace room. He could see, dimly, the wall outline of another door. It was in the direction the room had to be.

He took the spiral at tip-toeing pace, and covered the furnace room in twelve steps. He listened at the door, but could hear nothing through the fire door.

He began to edge the bolt lock from its track, and found he was having difficulty. He applied concerted pressure till it began to slide, then he knew he must fling it back as rapidly as possible, and shoot the door in its tracks, for if someone was on the other side, the surprise would be lost if they heard the lock slipping.

He steeled himself, shot the bolt and threw his weight against the door.

The fire door slid massively, caught, and slid in on its tracks, opening wide to the room. It was the Cat's den, as he had imagined, but it was empty.

The dull light of the flickering candle in its broken Chianti bottle told him someone had been there, however.

And a cigarette burned on the table's edge.

He stared at it for a long moment, wondering if Fabia had heard him coming into the factory, or had just run out when the door had squeaked. Then he heard a scuffle behind him, and tried to spin around to face whoever was there.

An arm as thick as a hawser slid around his neck, lifting him bodily from the floor. He kicked back, and his leg met something soft. He kicked again, and the choking slacked off slightly as a soprano cry of anguish spiraled toward the ceiling.

He used his elbows, and wiggled his neck in the tight grip, till he slipped free suddenly, and spun and drove the knife into the first obstacle it encountered.

His blade bit deeply, and he dragged down, opening a widening red rip in the flesh.

The soprano scream came again, and the dim shape in the shadows careened forward, clutching itself. It fell across the table, and tumbled to the floor, flopping onto its back.

Deek Cullen looked down; lying with her fingers thrust deep into the slashed breast, feeling her life heart-pump out, Terri died with eyes open.

CHAPTER SIX
Just Trust Me, Baby!

THE WALLS WERE COMING TUMBLING DOWN. The broad from the Settlement House, crazy bitch, she had the cops on him; Fabia had all the dough; Terri and Thumb were dead; and he was on the dodge again.

How had it all gone so wrong?

Had it been so slight a time ago that he had been lone top dog on the turf, walking and bopping the way he wanted? It had started wrong with that crazy nympho Pootzie, in the alley, and trying to avoid getting killed and hiding in Demoiselle's pad, and joining the Cats, and now all this...

He stood in the basement, and shook his head like a bull that has been struck by the matador and does not know which way is relief.

Then Fabia came down the steps. She took one look at the slashed body of Terri, and her eyes opened wide.

"Jeezus," she said. "I told her to watch for you...you bastard...you dirty bastard...that's two of them..."

Deek took a quick step toward her and grabbed her arm tightly. "Listen, I've got to get out of here, I've got to beat town, now where the hell's the dough? I swear to God I'll kill you if you don't tell me."

The maniacal expression in his eyes, the twist of his lips sent a shiver through the girl. She came toward him almost as if she wanted to get nearer the danger. "Deek, Deek," she murmured, "why did we have to end like this? We could have been so good together. Just you and me. Just you and me and all that dough, and no one else—"

Pootzie's intake of breath signaled her eavesdropping had paid off. Deek spun, still clutching Fabia's arm, and looked into the far corner of the dark room, where Terri had leaped out to attack him. Pootzie and Terri had arrived together.

"So you're gonna cop out on me, huh, Fabia?" Pootzie said. "Like hell you are." She drew back the pin of the zip gun and came out of the corner.

"You first, you sonofabitch!" she damned Deek. "You killed her, and she never had a chance. Now I'm gonna do it for you. I'm gonna put it right in the middle of that friggin' face of yours!"

She lifted the gun slightly, and drew back the heavy rubber band that would send the pin into the antenna barrel, driving the .32 slug into Deek's head.

Fabia slid out of Deek's grasp, and ducked slightly; Deek was too horribly fascinated by the small black dot of the zip gun's muzzle to notice.

The dark-haired girl came up from her crouch suddenly, and the switch blade was in her hand. Without a pause or break in rhythm, she brought the knife up and down, and drove it into Pootzie's chest. The rubber band jerked violently, the gun hand went up, and the slug buried itself with a rush and a roar in the ceiling.

Pootzie's eyes went wide and red, and she stared at the pillar of steel protruding from her chest.

"You…" she tried to condemn Fabia, and fell on her face, driving the knife deeper into her body.

Deek was petrified. When it began to wear off, he realized that Fabia DeLuca had saved his life. She had stopped Pootzie from blowing his skull apart.

"Why—" He began, but she cut him off by throwing herself into his arms. Her mouth came up to his, and his lips parted to receive her tongue. She ground her body against his, and pulled his head closer to her own with a death-grip in his hair. When she buried her face in his shoulder, her voice came to him softly, huskily. "I couldn't, I couldn't l-let her do it. I want you, Deek. I want you more than I want the money, or the gang, or any damn thing. I want you, and I want you to make love to me, alone, not with those other pigs around you. I need you, Deek. We can be awful good together. Please, Deek. Please, baby."

She ground her pelvis against him, and Deek felt the fury of his passion rising. It would be so easy. And she was the best woman he had ever had. She was hot and cold fire and all the rainbows and warm caves of a lifetime. He could maybe make it with her.

They'd have to split town; they'd have to hop a rattler and go out West, where they could set up and maybe start some crazy kind of normal life. It might be. It just might be.

She gasped with unsuppressed anguish, and cried, "Take me now, Deek. Take me on the sofa, Deek. Please!"

He lifted her, then, and carried her to the sofa. He laid her down and unbuttoned her jeans.

She rocked and writhed beneath him, and he felt the fires that had been stoked and banked by the day's torments, bursting forth. They rose higher and higher, and he tore at her feverishly, with insane passion.

"Oh-*hunch*..."

Then she lay silently in his arms, and he felt a great weariness bomb him. His eyes closed and he lay there atop her, still thrust deep within her, sleep coming like a great velvet curtain.

The pain wakened him.

He looked up. He was lying on his back. He felt very warm and very satisfied. It might be all right, after all. He would take Fabia, they would bury the bodies under the concrete in the basement. No one would ever find those vagabond girls who had been the sex gang members of the Cats. It would be Outsville, then, cutting fast on a train to nowhere, but cutting fast.

And maybe, in time, they'd be together more than just with their bodies. She was beautiful, and if they could ever kill the memories that lived between them... it was just a matter of trust.

Yeah, trust.

Trust from the day he was born. Trust for the world, and the people in it who had screwed him up and made him screw *them* up for revenge. It was all trust. Not enough of it.

But all that would change now.

Now he had a woman.

His own woman.

He would take her and go West, and they'd

settle someplace with all that dough, and make good. The pain really bothered him. He couldn't seem to swallow properly.

But he trusted her. That was what counted. She had a bad streak in her, all right, but so did he. He was a hungry type. But they'd made it together. It only took trust, and that would kill any hunger he had.

Something warm and moist was running stickily down his chest.

He found the difficulty with breathing was really bad now. He reached up, and touched his throat. His hand came away wet. He looked at his hand. Oh God, *no*!

Trust!

I'm hungry, he thought, I'm so damned hungry to make it, and make it on top. I'm hungry.

But someone is always hungrier, he mused, going red and dim in the sight, and seeing her there beautiful and dark and holding the knife that had cut his throat.

The knife that had been a friend to him. A good knife for anyone who needed a good one. His knife.

It was dark, suddenly. And quiet.

Nedra at ƒ:5.6

(An *Hommage* to Fritz Leiber)

I'M LOOKING AT THE PICTURES, but I don't believe it. I may just go have my eyes examined, or trade in that goddamned Leica and be done with it, but I don't—doubly do *not*—believe it. Listen: it's so weird, I didn't simply trust the raw negatives...I actually developed the bloody things, every frame.

Nedra's asleep in the bedroom, and well she *should* be after the monumental bout we staged tonight, and I'm almost afraid to go in and wake her. Oh, hell, it's just a trick of lighting, that's all, or something wrong with that damned Leica, or some crap got into the developer. But still...

Central Park uptown can be a strange and wonderful thing on an early spring day, but it wasn't a spring day. This was the middle of October, overcast, with the grass frantically struggling to stay green as it was trampled; with the trees whispering how clever they were to be dumping their leaves; with the sky siphoning down from a watery blue to a washed-out orange near the horizon. It was the Park on a day when all the nannies would rather have been in the apartments, with their white shoes off, drinking Pimm's Cups pilfered from their employer's home larders and watching *The Edge of Night* instead of perambulating their charges' perambulators. A week after the World Series, when the wormy little bookies who had lost their shirts when the Dodgers folded in five had crawled back into the topsoil till football season was under way. A sort of day that idles along, like a rolling hoop, just lightly jouncing over troublesome things like the canine Twinkies on the paths and the creepy gang kids looking for someone to mug, just going its way with an occasional shove or two.

That sort of day. And the people on the benches were nothing spectacular. Mostly old men and women, taking the sun—what there was left of it—and proud young mamas, showing their offspring to the folks.

It didn't look like the sort of day to be getting any good photos, but I decided to leg it around a few blocks of the Park and snap what there was. Overcast, just right, can get you some good candid color stuff. Sometimes.

Well, I was skirting the benches along in the Sixties, snapping one here and one there, catching a kid trying to stomp a dirty pigeon; catching a woman watching the sky to see if rain was coming and picking her nose at the same time; catching a bum twisted up like a foetus on a bench, with a copy of the *Wall Street Journal* over him for warmth. Nothing spectacular, but maybe it would look good in the darkroom.

It was just as I was passing the 79th Street underpass—you know, the part that takes you down to the boat basin—with the October wind snapping off the Hudson, tossing my hair around my head, making me wish I had worn my Aquascutum, when I spotted her.

Now, let me get this straight with you for a second. I've been a professional photographer for twelve years now. I'm thirty-five years old,

and I've snapped some of the wildest looking
women in the game. I've had Valerie Perrine
and Anne-Margret up on kitchen stools in front
of a white cyclorama sheet; I've posed Victo-
ria Vetri and Claudia Jennings and Charlotte
Rampling and Elsa Martinelli with and without their undies; I've done fashion layouts with
every *courant* breathtaker from The Shrimp to
Farrah Fawcett; even worked with the mythic
lust-dreams like Bettie Page and June Wilkin-
son and Irish McCalla and Anita Ekberg and
Vikki Dougan right at the end of their popular-
ity, before they vanished to wherever the great
beauties vanish to; I've seen more hundreds of
women in the bare, with their vitals exposed,
than any other dude with a planar I can think
of, excluding maybe Haskins, Avedon, de Di-
enes, Rotsler, Casilli, and a couple of others. So
stunning women aren't anything that special to
me, except maybe something to make a buck
off, if I can develop a set on them. What I'm saying is that Lauren Hutton isn't a coronary arrest
where I'm concerned if, as they say, you get my
drift.

I've made my living at cheesecake, when
there weren't "art" jobs or fashion layouts
handy, and I know damned well what *it* looks
like from every crotch-crazy angle you can think
of. So I should have known better…it shouldn't
have stopped me.

But that's just what she did. She stopped me
flat.

I just stared at her, sitting there in the afternoon, with the feeble sun overhead, and the
bench cool and green under her round bottom,

and the skirt up just a bit so I could see her knees didn't show bones, but were smooth and firm and flesh-colored.

She was like nothing I'd ever seen before. She was the answer to every cheesecaker's dream.

She just looked like she wanted to lie down on the grass.

With me. With the Good Humor Man. With the park attendant. With anybody.

You've probably seen pictures in magazines of girls like that. They just look more natural prone than supine. They seem to be saying with their eyes and their mouths and the lines of their bodies, "Let me lie down... I want to be horizontal." Well, she was like that, only more so, only much more so. She looked...well...the only word I could come up with was *hungry*. Yeah, that was it, *hungry*. She looked like she hadn't had a certain kind of meal in a helluva long time.

She was about five-feet-six, with hair that sent back the weak rays of the sun in a brilliant red explosion. Her hair wasn't the brassy, carroty red so many women think is hotcha; it was a delicate sort of amber, with highlights of black and streaks of deep crimson in it. It was hair that came down around her shoulders, and which she tossed out of her face with an eloquent twist of her shoulders.

I couldn't see what color her eyes were, because they were closed. She was sitting there with her hands in her lap, and her head tossed back and to the side slightly, as though she was sleeping.

It was a nippy day, and yet she wore no coat.

She had on a dark charcoal skirt and a pale blue poorboy jersey that stopped short of her upper arms. She must have been chilly as hell, but she wasn't shivering.

I was glad she hadn't worn that coat, because it gave me an uninterrupted view of her body. Now, ordinarily, in most women, no matter how skimpy or thin the clothing, there's still a portion of the anatomy you can't quite shape out in your mind. The under-breasts, the joint of the legs, the slide of the belly to the hips. But this girl was the next best thing to naked. Voluptuous. That was another word for her. Hungrily voluptuous. Voluptuously hungry. Either way, I could see the sharp molding of her breasts against the front of her jersey. I could see the sharp lines of indentation as the legs raced up to wide, rounded thighs, and plunged out of sight beneath her stomach. I could see her all, all of her, and it made me dizzy.

Have you ever experienced anything comparable? A roller coaster, doing forty push-ups, running a mile and a half in eleven minutes? All of them and others. This girl was the original Circe, the dyed-in-the-cotton-jersey siren.

I *had* to pose her.

I'm not bashful around women—my studio apartment has resounded long and loud to the outraged squeals of outraged models—but there was something about her that made me walk softly, on the balls of my feet, toward her.

Almost as though I'd tripped an electric eye as I approached, she sat up, and stared at me openly. I was stopped cold again. Her eyes were the most fantastic things I'd ever seen.

They were like the first movement of Rimsky-Korsakov's *Le Coq D'Or* transposed from sound to solid. They were like two green-hot chunks of emerald, bathed by the heat of an exploding sun, and smoldering, smoldering. They were all the invitations and all the ecstasies and all the open accusations of a woman who wants to make love no matter what the cost. They were alone in their category. They were more than merely eyes. Eyes see...these spoke.

"Hello," she said.

The voice couldn't have been more right for her had it been taped and recorded in the Muscle Shoals sound studios, with all the acoustical tricks of an echo chamber built into her vocal cords. The voice came at me and cracked me across the mouth. When that girl said hello, so help me God, I bit my lip.

"Hi...I'm, uh, my name is Paul Shores. I'm a, uh, photographer, and I'm, uh, I was watching you. Has anyone ever—"

She smiled, and it was the most complex smile I'd ever seen; working up from one corner of her very red mouth, and quickly overwhelming me; two rows of perfectly white teeth, with the little canines peeking out sharp and pointy. The smile brought two spots of color to her cheeks, and they looked almost unnatural in the setting of fine alabaster flesh. Her face was a composite, a study in red and pale pink. The kind of complexion they meant when they said peaches-and-cream, with none of the sick look of soggy peaches.

She finished my sentence for me: "Has anyone ever told me I was pretty enough to model?

Yes, Mr. Shores, any number of times, and any number of people."

The smile continued, as though, in some innocent, gentle, heartwarming way, she was mocking me, and I was so embarrassed I felt myself blushing. I quickly turned to leave, without even excusing myself.

I got one step away, and I felt her hand slip through my arm. "I'd love to pose for you," she said. I looked down at her.

She was serious, godammit! Absolutely serious about posing for a total stranger.

"But why?" I asked. "You don't know me from Ad—"

"Adam was much fatter than you." She replied, a pixie grin replacing the smile. "And besides, I think I can trust you. Any man who can afford a Leica doesn't have to pick up girls in the Park."

I was surprised that she recognized my camera, and even more surprised at her logic which, crazy as it was in an era when you can buy a hot Hasselblad on most street corners for sixty bucks, sounded logical. Nuts, but logical.

So we were off. In a little while most of my tongue-tootled attitude wore off, and I found I could speak almost coherently. I posed her in front of a statue of Pulaski; I posed her on a bench with her skirt up a bit; I posed her playing with two little children and their bastard-hound; I must have taken ten rolls of color on her before she took my hand and led me out of the Park.

"Where are we going?" I asked, feeling foolish as hell. A man is supposed to be master of these situations, and I felt like a Pekingese on a leash.

"You have a studio, don't you?" she inquired demurely.

I guess I bobbed my head stupidly in agreement, because the next time I took a breath, we were leaving the cab in front of my building, downtown, and the doorman was holding open the door for us, staring at her, just staring, staring.

The minute she got inside the door to my studio, the first thing she said was, "My name is Nedra. May I take off my clothes?"

What the hell do you say? Sure you can take off your clothes.

So she did. Or started to, anyhow. "Let me take some snaps of you undressing," I said, knowing damned well few girls who aren't pro models will let you shoot that kind of thing; don't ask me why; maybe because they're the sexiest shots in the world.

"Okay," she said, and started in.

She stepped up onto the model's pedestal I have in the studio, and began taking off that pale blue poorboy jersey. Now, hold it a second.

You'd better understand this.

She wasn't doing a strip. None of that chubby housewife trying to hold onto her fat-assed hubby by learning to belly dance or excite him with "imaginative sex" fantasies bullshit.

She was doing it *for* me, of course; I'd asked her if I could take the shots, for God's sake! But she wasn't trying to do it *to* me; do you know what I'm saying here? There's nothing more cornball than some female trying to pull a Theda Bara, batting her eyelashes and all turkey-flapping with what "family-programmed" television and sexploitation films have conned her into believing is a turn-on. Jesus, it's a puker.

No, there wasn't any of that going down. She was just *doing* it…for me…*at* me…but not purposely *to* me…

Click!

The sweater was stuck in the top of her skirt. She yanked at it, and it came loose, dragging up the top of her black lace panties, too. My eyes had trouble focusing on the camera. She pulled the sweater off, letting her arms go back and her breasts jut out at me, and the sweater fell down behind her, off the pedestal, onto the floor. Her breasts were just as I'd imagined them in the sweater.

Click!

They were large and round, and they stayed where they were. But then, they must have been where they were all the time, because, you see, she didn't have on a brassiere. Then she unfastened the catch on the side of the skirt.

Click!

I watched her, and the thought that this girl was going a lot further than was expected for just a little modeling hit me right in the head. Was she a nympho, who let every guy pick her up? Was she a psycho? What was the score?

To hell with Click!

I dumped the camera and moved toward her. She stood there, naked but for the black lace panties, and her breath was coming with difficulty, rasping in and out faintly. Her hands were quivering. Then I was beside her, and I slid my arms around her. She was on the pedestal, and I locked hands behind her, the smooth curve of her strange and wonderful to me. I let my hands slide up to the small of her back, down to the indentations where her legs joined her trunk. Was this girl real? Was all this happening to me? Then she bent, and she kissed me.

Then she bit my lip. She bit me right where I'd bitten myself, and I felt the trickle of salty warmth, and her tongue smoothed over it, and I felt her shudder.

I stood up, from where I'd slumped against the pedestal, and let my hand slide under her legs at the knees, the other behind her back, turning her to me, lifting her, cradling her in my arms.

Then we were in the bedroom, and she was on the white sheets, whiter than they could ever hope to be, with that flame hair and those hell-green eyes staring at me.

Without movement, without time, without the feeling of penetration, it was done, her voice dying stillborn, and her hands scraping terribly at my back.

My God! It was unbelievable.

Neither one of us thought about rest, or food, or anything else, much less photography, till an hour ago. I woke up and looked across at her. Even after the passion-effort I'd expended, and the fatigue coursing through me, she still looked untouched and magnificent; her hair an amber aurora sprayed out across the rumpled pillow, her eyes closed, and her breath shallow. I felt weak in every muscle, every joint. My back was ripped from the sharpness of her nails, and my lips were raw. It had been so unlike any other thing I knew, I couldn't let her go. I had to have Nedra around all the time.

I lay there for a few minutes, and then the excitement of those films I'd taken earlier sent me out of bed. I grabbed my bathrobe and got the rolls of film from my case, flipped the last one out of the camera, and made for the darkroom.

They developed nicely, and they were clear as hell. Some of the best shots I'd ever taken. I'm standing here looking at them now.

There's just one thing wrong with them. It must be a trick of the light or something...or something...

But here are the pictures I took in the Park. Here's the fountain, and the two children with the hound, and the bench, and the trees and the sky and the river and the grass, and everything...

But no Nedra.

Yeah. That's right. Everything else in perfect focus but there isn't a sign of her in any of the shots. I've got the pedestal, and the backdrop and the apartment and the shadows, but no shadow of Nedra. In fact, no Nedra at all.

But she's no figment of my imagination. That's for sure. A girl with a horizontal mind like that *couldn't* be imaginary. I just don't believe in anything like that.

Well, when she wakes up, I'll go in and just ask her what she's...oh, hi!

I was just coming in to wake you. Say, look at these crazy pix I shot of you today. Aren't they screwy? You just didn't photograph. You know, I was thinking all sorts of crazy stuff, and listen to this, this is the craziest thing yet.

I started to think, and the only kind of person I could think of who doesn't reflect in a mirror, or who won't show up on a photo...now I know it's crazy, it must have been the light or something, but...

Nedra!

The Bohemia of Arthur Archer

(as by "Cordwainer Bird")

STANDING OUTSIDE THE DOOR of the Greenwich Village cold-water flat, Arthur Archer—blond and tall—turned to Burt Simmons—short and sweaty—and asked: "How're chances of getting laid tonight?"

From inside the apartment could be heard the mingled mangling of party voices. Bert let the corner of his mouth curl, and he said: "Five to one, Artie boy. If there's five girls here tonight...you'll get one.

"The odds go up proportionately; nine-to-two, thirteen-to-three, hell, you understand."

Arthur grinned his which-way-is-the-meat grin, and nodded. "I understand." Bert knocked on the door.

It slid open of its own weight, unlocked, and Arthur Archer got his first look at a Bohemian party in the Village.

It was straight out of Dante. Or perhaps Lewis Carroll. Or *someplace*, anyhow. Arthur stopped just inside the door, as Bert brushed past screaming, "Deidre, *baaa*by!" He let the dull-faced girl with the poodle-cut take his summer hat, and he stared.

It was a wild mixing of color and sound. There were at least a hundred people crammed into the apartment, and more, Arthur was sure, were in the other rooms. Bert had told him earlier: "This was an old hotel, but they divided it up into apartments. Deidre's place has eight bedrooms, so if you latch onto something good, don't wait till the end of the evening to drag her back to bed…because they usually pair off and seek solitude about two, three o'clock in the A.M."

And Arthur, fresh from college and home for the summer with his fraternity brother Bert, wanted very *much* to latch onto a girl.

So he let his gaze slide around the room, taking in all the confusion and madness of the party. One fellow, with hair that hadn't been cut, obviously, since Barbara Fritchie hung her flag out the window, was doing an involved African war-step in the middle-center of the dimly lit room. He was going, "Hoo *ha*, hoo *ha*, ugga, ugga, ugga!" and mincing about on his toes, arms flailing wildly.

A second joker was perched cross-legged atop the tv, a bath towel wrapped around his head, swami-fashion, and telling the fortunes of three gigglingly attentive girls—all buck-toothed or wearing horn-rimmed glasses. *These are girls? These are people?* Arthur thought in amazement.

A girl with a twitch, and a ponytail nestling in the small of her back, was sitting in the center of a group of people, reading from the works of Edith Sitwell, in a deep and emphatic voice, each word laced with significance.

Arthur found all this hard to believe. He was a college man, he was reasonably mature, and he was sure he had winnowed the chaff of fable from the wheat of life's reality. But here was a cliché coming true. He'd *heard* of Bohemian parties, but this seemed to be a tourist's dream. Abruptly, he felt Bert's hand on his bicep, and turned. Bert had a young girl in tow—one with lips that were so thin they looked as though an artist had lined them in with charcoal; glasses black and forbidding; a chest that was the nearest thing to inverted he had ever seen on a woman; eyes that bugged so, they looked as though they were attempting to leave her head, just to say hello.

"Art, this is Deidre…this is her place. She threw the party."

The goggle-eyed goblin extended a hand, grabbed Art's own, and crushed it systematically. "Individualist!" she said, much too loudly.

"Pardon?" Art asked.

"Said individualist! Want you to be individualist! Make self at home. Worry about nothing. Leave everything to me. Be gay. Have fun. Read you later."

And she was gone, lost in the maze of flesh, sound and scent.

Arthur felt as though he had left his head in a cocktail shaker for a while. "Does, uh, does she always talk in telegram-talk that way?" he demanded of Bert, confusedly.

Bert grinned fatuously. They were fraternity brothers, and he had seen things come so easy to the tall, blond Archer, he was inwardly pleased when someone or something confused him. "Uh-uh. Last year it was epigrams. She'd wander up when you came in, and say, 'What is it that an old man watches, that a young girl can have, that a koala bear cannot understand?'"

"Well, what's the answer?"

Bert spread his hands. "A good time. That's what she told me—like I was dumb or something—just a good time. Then she says, 'Have one,' and walks away to her other guests."

"This makes sense to you?"

"C'est ca," Bert replied, grinning wider still. "Look, brother Arthur, we got into this party only because I used to run with some of the artists from the Village before I went off to State to become buddy-buddy with you. So take what you see at face value, don't question, and hope you wind up with a face that has some value." He wandered away looking for the bar. Or the jug. Or the sneaky pete. Or anybody who had wet lips.

Arthur watched the mad goings-on in the living room for a few more minutes, and then decided to see what was happening in the other eight rooms of the monstrous apartment.

Several doors were closed, and when he attempted to open one—obviously a bedroom—he was greeted by a shout of, "Shut the goddam door...we're busy!"

He smiled hopelessly, wishing *he* were busy, and went down the long hall, in the direction of noise, music and whistles.

It was a dining room, but the table had been cleared to the side, where people sat and stood on it. The crowd was even larger here and he immediately saw why.

A girl was dancing in the center of the room. The lights were down to one wall-bracket, casting a yellow glow, and someone had turned on a calypso record. The girl was moving slowly, sensually, to the beat of the drums, the sound of the fife, the plunk of the guitar.

She was obviously looped to the ears, but on her—it looked just the other side of wonderful.

All the rest of these characters had seemed like maniacs, Bohemians or not. (And he was quite certain he despised Bohemianism!) They had seemed like oddball, pointless crap.

But this one wasn't pointless.

Uh-*uh*! She was pointy as a hound-dog.

He stared at her open-eyed. She was almost as tall as he, with hair tied into the usual ponytail. But hair that was a starkly inviting blue-black, and ponytail twisted painstakingly into a spiral. It hung to her narrow shoulders, and set off the tan of her face beautifully. She wore a tight black sweater that threatened to burst its seams at any instant, a white skirt that swirled as she stepped, lifting high to reveal slim legs and white thighs above the tightly-gartered stocking-tops, and high heels. He ran back up from the feet to the head, stopping for a long moment at the chest.

This for the entire summer! Arthur thought tightly.

He shoved his way through the crowd, watching her flashing legs, her gorgeous body. He came to the front edge of the group of stamping, whistling, chortling Bohemians and watched her face as she moved. She seemed almost unaware anyone was in the room with her. Looped, yes, but something more. Her eyes were the deepest black he'd ever seen. Slanted just a bit—Eurasian parents?—and the cheekbones were high. Her mouth was a full, subtle, hungry-looking thing, and she wore that rarity, light purple lipstick—and wore it well.

"Who is she?" Arthur inquired of a dumpy, curlyheaded boy next to him.

"That's Christie Mayland," he answered, as though the serf had just asked who the King was.

He turned away from the curlyhead, continued watching her. Christie, when drunk, was an only slightly less appealing entity than when sober. And to Arthur, she was *more* appealing. Her eyes had acquired—with the liquor—a sheen, a depth, a more irresistible hunger than before. She had the unconscious habit of running her pink, pink tongue-tip over her full lips. Christie was moving sinuously, her hands live things, exploring her body, motioning and beckoning. Her small feet moved in involved steps, and her hair bobbed like a caged reptile in its ponytail binding.

"Man, she is *great*!" Arthur murmured.

"Yeah. She's a stripper in a club down here in the Village," the dumpy curlyhead inserted.

Arthur tossed him a fast glance, not wanting to take his eyes from the rounded mounds of her breasts. "It figures."

The beat of the music swelled, and Arthur remembered a scene like this at a fraternity stag party one night, when they had gotten a stripper drunk, and hot, and they'd clamored for Arthur to dance with her. "Sock it to her, Artie! Dance, Artie! Go, go, go, go!" And Artie, slightly tight himself, had danced with the stripper till they were both nude.

This was the same thing. With a roomful of

Bohemians. But still...

The guitars beat over and over in repetition, and Arthur stood at the edge of the crowd, hardly realizing he was inching into the cleared space where the beautiful Christie Mayland danced. Christie moved carefully—still stoney drunk!—arching her back, switching her full hips. She had a close, tight walk, and the skirt swirled with every movement, till she grasped it and pulled it tight to her legs, sheathing them, so every muscular ripple shivered the material.

She was getting set to pull it up over her head, start her strip routine, and then Arthur stepped in, took her in his arms, and whirled her in traditional dance-steps.

Everyone in the room groaned. They had thought they were going to see more of Christie's bare flesh. Now her dance had been cut short right at the hot part. Arthur wasn't quite sure why he had done it; somehow he couldn't see her revealing all that loveliness to a roomful of schnooks.

That stuff is for me only, he thought, spinning the suddenly limp Christie in his arms.

"Come on, let her finish!" one fellow yelled, but Arthur gripped her all the closer, feeling the rounded firmness of her warm breasts pressing through his shirt.

Then, Christie began to struggle. She squirmed for release, and finding it more difficult than she had thought, brought her high-heeled foot down on Arthur's foot. He howled and stepped back.

"Goddam conformisht!" she yelled, her beautiful mouth opening to show white, even teeth.

"You aren't even a li'l bit Bohemyun! Goddam conformisht, breakin' up my act!"

She stepped toward him, her slap formed and ready to be delivered. Arthur took a half-step backward, and grabbed her as she swung. She tumbled into his arms, cold faint, and limp as an old shoestring.

"Which way is an empty bedroom, where I can toss her to sleep?" Arthur demanded. Nobody answered. They glared at him unhappily.

Exasperated, Arthur shoved through the crowd, back down the long hall, till he came to an open door. It was one of the many bedrooms—and empty. He kicked it open, angled inside with Christie still inert in his arms, kicked it shut, and fumbled in the darkness along the wall for a light switch. When he found it, he clicked light into the room, and tossed Christie unceremoniously on the bed. Her skirt billowed as she bounced on the mattress, and settled about her hips, the long, delicious legs revealed in their nylon sheaths.

Arthur locked the door and flopped into a chair.

Here was a problem of the first magnitude.

As if to accentuate it, Christie sat up blearily, her arms straight back behind her in support, and mumbled, "I wouldn' do it with you if you were the onny guy in thish whole worl'... goddam conformisht!" And flopped back dead-asleep.

Arthur dragged a cigarette from his shirt pocket, and lit it. The trouble seemed to be—as far as he could tell—she didn't consider him Bohemian enough. He wasn't unwashed and barefoot, bearded and unkempt. Nor was he bristling with esoteric knowledge and/or egomania. He was just a nice, average guy who wanted a short snort roll in the hay.

For the whole summer.

And to get it, he was going to have to cultivate Christie Mayland. Who didn't seem to want this particular farmer to cultivate her.

He sank back in the chair, dejected, and waited for the gorgeous hunka flesh on the bed to get sober enough for reasoning.

About three A.M. Christie came to. Not sober, just conscious. Arthur was huddled in the chair...he had never much liked the idea of assaulting an unconscious woman. She sat up, her eyes asparkle, and grinned at him widely.

"My li'l conformisht baby!" she cried, and struggled out of bed toward him. The rest of the apartment had settled into silence hours before, and the pat-pat of her feet was the only sound in the place.

Arthur watched her archly as she came toward him, and grunted half in pleasure, half in weariness as she plopped into his lap. "You ain't musch," she mumbled, "but you're all I got tonight..."

She lowered her face to his, took his head between her slim fingers, and kissed him full on the mouth, her hot tongue darting in like a firebrand, and her lips working on his.

Instinctively he let his arms slide about her waist, but before she could be fully circled, she was off his lap, standing in the middle of the room, yawning, stretching till her sweater strained; she raised on tip-toe.

"Oh! A radio," Christie bubbled, seeing a portable on the vanity table. "I wanna finish my dansh!"

She turned it on, and the insistent beat of a popular rock 'n' roll melody filled the room. She took up her dance, just where she had left off before. With her skirt.

She danced a few rocking steps, her walk more a burley switch than a step-movement, then with one violent movement she pulled up the hem of her skirt; above her knees, clinging to her thighs, holding it there with one hand wrapped tightly in the fabric. Her legs were sun-tanned and supple, colored by the sheer nylon of her hose. Delicate feet and full rich thighs, moving whitely and quickly.

The nylons were held up by garters, and as she moved, she took prancing steps, lifting her leg high, bending the knee quickly, and bringing the foot down hard. The nylons started to slip at her movements, and she paused to run her cupped hands up the extreme length of the leg, tightening the hose. It drew a sharp breath from the sweating Arthur Archer.

She had gotten to a point where dancing still clothed was confining, and Arthur waited expectantly. She was used to semi-nudity on the stage...and she had lost the habit of under-things. It was a fantastic picture—a study in blue-black and white. Arthur felt himself sinking into the mood, going down and around and inward with the sight of gorgeous Christie May-land.

The drums' insistent beat started Christie bumping her stomach, grinding her hips. Abruptly, the dress seemed horribly confining, and she pulled it up over her head, throwing the ponytail from its clasp, letting the hair fall full and blue-black around her face and shoulders.

Arthur's breath caught in his throat. She was, indeed, stark-naked, save her black lace brassiere, which held her high, full breasts closely and tightly.

Vibrating to the rhythms, Christie spun and ducked, her legs wide, her arms high. She continually wetted her lips, looking toward Arthur with hunger and passion.

Her hands slid slowly up her legs, across her thighs, over her belly, and under her breasts. She encountered the slight material of the bra with her fingers and instantly divested herself of the garment. It was one that fastened in front, and it came away with a sibilant *whiss*! and she was uncovered, save the high-heels and nylons.

Then she finished the movement interrupted by the bra. Her hands lovingly, gently, tenderly, then more tightly, more ferociously, cupped the breasts, pulled them up, and her hand swept away, up to her face, where they ran palms-flat across the planes of her cheeks, back to lift her hair away in a wild movement.

Her breasts quivered, and the tiny pink nipples rose from her burning touch. She strained toward the blond boy in the chair, and Arthur could feel molten slag coursing up and down his body, drenching his thighs in sweat.

With a little moan she leaped in the air, came down spinning, her breasts moving with every action, the nipples alert and standing forth.

Then she moved toward Arthur. "I'm gonna regret thish in the mornin', but right now I don't give a damn!" she said, running her tongue over his lips, leaving them shining.

Arthur had almost forgotten he was smoking; the cigarette had burned so close to his face as he watched, hardly realizing it was there, that it sent smoke into his eyes, bringing tears, charring his lips.

He yanked the butt from his mouth and crushed it under his heel, standing to meet her as he did it. She came to him, and her body was a live thing, all flame and silk, thrust against him. He felt every ridge and depression of her. The smoldering twin fires of her breasts, the matted heat of her lower body, the smooth expanse of her stomach, and he felt like screaming. It was all the women he had ever bedded and more—it was all the women he had ever *dreamed* of bedding.

His hands started low, cupped, and moved over her buttocks, into the small of her back, up and around, and winding, till her had her breasts in his hands, and he lowered his perspiring face to them.

The soft nipples tautened under his lips, and suction brought them standing again, with the passion of what was to come building up from her bowels, enveloping them both.

Then she leaped away.

He stood there panting, watching her. She stepped toward him again, and he grabbed her, pulling her close by her hair. She wrapped one long leg around his, and ground herself into him. And her lips were mad, insane things, demanding to be bruised, bloodied.

Then he felt her working on the buttons of his shirt, and eased back. She caught one of them, and in his anxiety he brushed her hand away, ripped the shirt loose. The button bounced to the floor, but he didn't hear it. In a matter of seconds she had him naked also, and they moved carefully, closely, hotly together.

The song ended suddenly, and they stood staring at each other, their breath coming hard and deep. He stared down the entire length of her, perspiration giving her suntanned flesh a gloss that brought water to his mouth.

He moved in on her, put his lips to her bare shoulder and sucked, biting slightly. When he drew away, a red patch had been left, and she stood there, head thrown back, mouth open, and eyes shut, breathing deeply.

The silence of the room became oppressive for a moment, and then, as naturally, as logically, as if they had known each other since the dawn of time, they were on the bed, moving in a tight motion.

Then they were deep into each other, their limbs entwined, and the act began. The heaving and tossing of boats on stormy seas, the crack of lightning, the smashing of the Great Wall of China, all were there, locked in them as they moaned in each other's ears.

The next number on the radio was a quiet love song, but it didn't quite fit the mood of action in the room.

"Oh, Great God, no! Of all the creeps I could've shacked-up with... I had to wind up with *you*!"

Arthur turned over, feeling muggy but contented, and saw the outraged and rumpled face of Christie Mayland, hair tumbled and eyes bright, staring down at him. She was propped on one hand, and her eyes spat vehemence. "That'll teach me to get plastered!"

"What's the matter, Christie?" he asked, hoping she wouldn't remember she didn't like him.

"Don't call me Christie, you goddam jerk of a conformist!" She spat the word "conformist" as though it were "leprosy" or "dog catcher." This was the problem to end all problems. A Bohemian stripper, who didn't like him—good lay though he had been—because he wasn't stinking, barefoot, and loaded with arcane minutiae.

So Arthur Archer, uncomfortable being in the Village to begin with, lay there for an hour listening to Christie's tirade against him. It seemed she wasn't disturbed because he had made her, it was just that he was such a schloonk of a bourgeois conformist—no Bohemianism to him at all—she couldn't face her friends, the artists and authors.

"So I'll become a Bohemian," Arthur interrupted, just saying it so she might lay off him.

"You? You a Bohemian. Don't make me vomit!"

"But, I ..."

"I never want to see you again ...you, you, you *creep*!" she concluded, her rage mounting till it moved her hand. The fist slammed around, belted a beaut into Arthur's jaw, and Christie was long-legged out of bed.

"Ooooh," she moaned, looking down. "And with the nylons on yet! My last pair!"

He nursed his jaw, watching her dress quickly (and she *still* was the sexiest animal he'd ever met!), and then tried a timorous, "So long, Christie baby. See you soon," as she flounced out the door.

All he got for his trouble was a "Humphh!" and the door slammed. Arthur felt like the very hell.

That was the Stuff-For-The-Entire-Summer: walking away.

Then he remembered what he had said, groping for a way to keep Christie handy. He had said, "So I'll become a Bohemian…"

It had only been an idle thought, but suddenly everything dawned, and he saw how he could capture Christie. How he could keep that Summer Stock for himself.

It was a nauseating idea, but he knew he could be a great actor when the case demanded.

But first he had to do some research.

He had gotten her address from Deidre. He had gotten briefed and directed by Bert…who was utterly confused by the entire affair. He had done the reading (almost twenty-five books in one week). He had gone down to the Village night after night, sitting in Rienzi's and Nick's, and picked up the local color, the manner of speech, the topics of discussion. He had gotten in with a fellow at a record shop, and painfully absorbed the music. He had bought the necessary attire for the situation. And now he was ready.

His head burst with Hemingway and Mencken and Proust and T.S. Eliot and Colette and Tolk-

ien and de Tocqueville and Kafka and Strind-
berg and Cassirer and Sartre. Plus a hundred
others whose work he had nibbled and sampled
and scanned. His whistling now ran to Ives and
Bach and Bartok and Mahler and Berlioz and
Vivaldi and Orff and Scarlatti. He could spot a
Brueghel or a Monet or a Dufy or a Kandinsky
or a Wyeth or a Picasso at eighty paces. He knew
the plot of every play, off- and on-Broadway, for
the last five years.

He was, in memories and thought, a Bohemian.

He could spout with the best of them.

And when he appeared at the door of Christie Mayland's fourth floor walkup apartment, he
looked like this:

He wore Bermuda walking shorts, sandals,
a green beret, a beard of two weeks growth, no
shirt but a rep tie knotted carefully about his
throat.

Christie opened the door. Arthur was about
to say, "Well, am I Bohemian enough now?"

"You're ridiculous!" Christie spat, and
slammed the door in his face.

It had been a round of parties, one after another, with the hope he'd see Christie. But after
the thirteenth one, he had become so involved
with the groups of Bohemians in the Village,
so taken with their discussions, he wasn't particularly interested anymore. At first he went
to them with Bert, but then Bert began staring at him oddly—and also, Bert wasn't *really*
anything more than a conformist—so he went
alone. After a short time, the company of the

buck-toothed, ponytailed, black turtleneck sweatered, unkempt Bohemians seemed to be natural.

He moved out of Bert's home, got himself a furnished room in the Village—determined to make it with Christie; and after all, somehow *enjoying* this Bohemian life of sitting around Rienzi's, drinking cappuccino, smoking Turkish cigarettes, discussing the significance of Robert Graves or the worthwhileness of Redgrave in *Tiger at the Gate*. It was beginning to be a pleasure.

And finally, Christie showed up. He was in the midst of a group of younger Villagers, explaining how his novel—the one in progress—was to be a scathing denunciation of the ironclad mind of the conformist college man.

She saw him, and her jaw dropped. He watched her from the corner of his eye as she came toward them, and as he watched her long-legged stride, the subtle whispering of nylon against nylon, flesh against flesh, he suddenly realized the past month or so had wrought a great change in him. The pleasures of the flesh were important, of course, but they were secondary, actually. His pleasure could be taken with any one of these interesting horned-rim glasses and dark girls clustered about his feet.

He wasn't really any longer interested in Christie. She was beautiful, all right, but that was more for the conformist…for the college man. She wasn't…she just wasn't…

He couldn't quite put it into words.

He was talking to a short, dumpy, curly headed girl, and fished his cigarette holder from his pocket, took a butt from behind his ear, leaned toward the girl for a light.

Abruptly, Christie's hand jutted over the head of one of the acolytes, and she was offering him the flame of her lighter.

He accepted it without looking around, and when she said huskily, "Hello... Art... I heard you were living down here now."

He looked up at her. Beautiful. That was all. Just absolutely luscious gorgeous without-comparison beautiful. Such a pity.

"Don't you say hello?" she asked.

"Not too often..." he replied, and then it all summed up so clearly; for once Arthur was able to express what he meant simply, and he knew what was wrong with her:

"You aren't Bohemian enough!"

He turned back to the dumpy, curlyheaded girl—who would have been happy, nay overjoyed, to go to bed with this rising light of the Village Bohemian crowd—and resumed telling her about the existentialist novel he was writing. Down here. Down here in the Village... where he belonged.

Where a lay like Christie was just too bourgeois.

Jeanie With The Bedroom Eyes

HE WATCHED HER UNDRESS in the front window of the department store.

Don Kingery had *been* watching her do it for almost a month now, and he wasn't sure he could take it much longer.

Her name was Jean Belamonte and she was a model. What they called in the trade, a "bedwarmer." He watched the smooth play of muscles on her slim arms as she folded the dressing-gown across the bottom of the bed.

Tossing her almost blond hair in a careless gesture, she prepared to go to bed for the day.

He watched with a strange (but all too frequent these days) dryness in his mouth as she turned down the covers. Her body was slim and tall, yet voluptuous; a marvelous stereotype of a Grecian statue. Jean Belamonte's skin was a rare combination of pink and gold—It fairly shone in the fluorescent glow of the overhead DayLights banked around the inside of the store window.

He watched her raise one neatly-turned leg, the edge of her prim, but still curve-hugging, nightgown sliding up the firm calf, and clinging just below the knee. His mouth filled suddenly with saliva, and he felt his knees deliquesce beneath him, melting Popsicles. It was almost more than a normal man could take!

"Oh, Jeanie, Jeanie, Jeanie…" he mumbled to himself.

A woman in the crowd next to him turned an outraged glance his way. "You certainly don't *know* that hussy, do you, young man?" she wanted to know.

Kingery didn't even bother looking at the woman. He knew what she would look like: thin-lipped, pale, hawk-beaked, and not even attractive enough to carry the bedpan to Jean Belamonte's window resting-place. A sour grapes viewer who thought the show-window advertisement for ComfeeSnooze Mattresses was immoral—even though it had been okayed by the police.

"No, ma'am," he sighed, keeping his eyes on the inches of silk-covered loveliness disappearing beneath the sheets, "unfortunately I only know her by sight."

Not only had Don Kingery been getting used to the sight of voluptuous Jean Belamonte taking repose in that window, but he had persuaded the general manager to keep the display going. Ten days was the usual run of a store window display. But Jean had been drawing crowds for over a month. There was just *something* about her. That *something* was causing Don Kingery's metabolism to do odd things. Like back-flips and deep knee-bends.

He turned away with a dejected twist of the hand and walked back into Pomeroy's Department Store.

In the window, the bedclothes heaved slightly over the full, thirty-eight inch bust of Jean Belamonte as she fell quickly asleep.

Before the eyes of a large, mixed crowd.

(55 hungrily admiring males. 26 enviously

damning females.)

Don Kingery was twenty-nine years old, was six foot two, with deep brown hair and eyes that matched. He had the build of a half back and the instincts of a predator. He had no trouble with women, for all of the above reasons—and a few more. He had his own bachelor apartment, and was second-in-command of the Pomeroy floorwalkers. He had been with Pomeroy's almost eight years and during that time the flood of salesgirls, women buyers, lady customers (both married and single), models and just stray females that had crossed his path had not swerved him from the art of living-alone. He had been a prime purveyor of the theory of the sanctity of bachelor singularity that cried: Love 'Em, Lay 'Em and Leave 'Em.

This he had done successfully. But the past month, this month with Jeanie Belamonte sliding down to snooze in the front window every morning at 9:30, had been the hardest he'd ever known.

At first he'd ignored the girl. All right, perhaps she *was* the best "bed-warmer" in the business; perhaps she *had* been doing this work for six years; perhaps she *was* a gorgeous woman! So what? That's what Don Kingery had wanted to know—so what?

So he had found out. The hard way.

One morning he had come in early, and had passed by the models' dressing booths. He passed the dressing room where Jeanie changed into her nightgown and bathrobe. The curtain had not slipped completely across on its hooks, and the brief space through which he had been able to see held a fascinating tableau.

He had stopped stock still, the boutonniere on its way to his button hole frozen in mid-motion.

Jeanie had been admiring herself in the full-length mirror. She had been sliding her skirt up her body slowly, letting the full, curving taper of leg and thigh come into sight cautiously. Don had watched as she drew the clinging fabric up, up, till the top of her hose had been exposed, the garter leading to soft, dark blue panties revealed, the V where her torso met her legs uncovered. He hadn't realized his breath was caught in his throat till he had turned red and began coughing.

She had heard him then, and only gotten a fleeting glimpse of his back as he had run like the wind down the back stairs to the bargain basement.

Since that day, Don Kingery had had but one problem:

How to get Jeanie Belamonte out of the bed in the window—and into his own!

It took him three more weeks to get up the nerve. During that time he had escorted to his bachelor bed (a) a redheaded school teacher who had dropped into Pomeroy's to complain about a defective orange squeezer she had purchased, (b) a hot-blooded sweater model from Teen Toggery who had a penchant for exercising her muscles in strange ways and (c) a petulant but bed-frenzied saleswoman of novelty marshmellow products, from Wichita, Kansas.

They had all been vital—yet tasteless. Not one of them was anything more than a dim shadow the morning after. All Don Kingery—he of the broad shoulders, dark wavy hair and dark wavy eyes—could see was the face and form of Jeanie Belamonte. He always thought of the name with an *ahhhhh!* and a licking of the lips.

He finally asked her.

He opened the door to the window, and before the amazed eyes of the crowd, he entered the fully-fitted bedroom. He was oblivious of the gawping pedestrians.

Jeanie was stretched out full-length under the covers, as usual. He could see the sharp outlines of her beautiful legs, even through the blanket bulk. The heat of the DayLights was almost oppressive, but a fan hidden under the bed kept the window cool and refreshing.

He paused for a second and imagined the nakedness that lay under the covers, under the sheets, under the nightie.

It was too much for him. He cleared his throat.

Jeanie Belamonte sat bolt upright. The sheet fell away from her and Don Kingery drew in a deep, sharp breath at the exposed beauty of her breasts. High, finely-molded half-globes, they strained impatiently at the thin, nearly-transparent fabric of the nightgown.

Wildly, the thought ran through his head: *That* can't *be the nightie she wore when the cops okayed this display! It can't be—or we would've been banned cold!*

Her deep turquoise eyes snapped open in fear. But he didn't see them. He was too busy looking at the rest of her. She had actually been asleep—asleep before a milling crowd—and this invasion of her privacy (*privacy? Good Lord!* he thought) had frightened her.

He was about to tell her not to worry, when he saw her eyes.

They were fantastic! They were unbelievable! He couldn't control himself. He felt not only the heat of his body rising, not only the color of his body rising, but his body...

He didn't ask her just then.

He turned quickly and rushed out of the window, slamming the door behind himself. He strode quickly to his office and slammed the door. Two slams, no fouls. He told his secretary—over the intercom—not to disturb him for an hour.

They had been the most limpid, most appealing, most hungry and lascivious eyes he had ever seen. Kingery had been in the Marines; had been in Casablanca and Tokyo, been in Nevada and Hollywood. Yet he had *never*—absolutely *never*—seen anything like them. He had romanced visiting movie stars—in the book department autographing ghost-written biographies. He had slept with man-starved saleswomen on the road for weeks and frenetic teenaged salesgirls anxious for promotion. He had wined, dined, and danced (in all positions) with women of all types and all conditions.

But the eyes of Jean Belamonte, these unbelievably demanding turquoise eyes with the messages of fire that leaped and sparkled, sent all other memories to the lowest level of remembrance. They were—and there were no

other words possible—unquestionably the ulti-
mate in that fabled type:

BEDROOM EYES!

Don Kingery's mind used the capitals automatically. For two weeks he saw those eyes swim-
ming in his dreams. Unquiet and unrewarding
dreams that left him sweating and snarled in his
bedclothes. The other women he had coveted,
faded to nothingness in his interest.

He had to have Jeanie Belamonte!

Finally, after the sweating and the dry mouth
and the everlastingly damned hunger in his
loins could contain him no longer, it became an
obsession. He *would* have her!

He was afraid to try approaching her for a
date while she was in the window. Aside from
the fact that he had been warned by his superior
about going in there when Jeanie was pounding
her ear on the ComfeeSnooze, he was afraid of
himself. He wasn't quite sure he might not leap
on her, actually *frothing*!

He waited till she left the window at 5:30 in
the evening. Three nights in a row he watched
her enter the dressing room, swathed in her
bathrobe, the terrycloth clinging and partially revealing the alabaster rise of her breast
mounds. Three nights in a row he watched her
emerge in figure-hugging sweater and skirt.
Once she even paused to straighten her seams.
With caressing motions she ran her hands up
her fine legs, the nylon whispering beneath her
fingers.

Her long legs were all the more appealing en-
cased in sheer nylon, blanketed from sight by
the tight skirt.

Her almost-blond hair drawn back into a long ponytail, the tilt of her small nose, the high rise of her cheekbones, the full spaciousness of her pointed breasts, all these made him go margarine-melty.

Jeanie Belamonte had been made for love.

But most of all—those eyes. Everyone else seemed to have developed empty sockets in their heads when he thought about the bedroom eyes of Jeanie Belamonte.

On the fourth evening, he approached her.

"Miss Belamonte?" he inquired. His voice was calm. He had practiced for weeks in front of his apartment mirror. But his guts were winding and unwinding within him. He suspected if she answered, his legs would rubberize and zing out from under him.

"Yes?" her tones, her stretched syllables, and the arch of her eyebrows were quizzical.

"I'm Don Kingery. You must remember me, I'm the fellow who—"

"—the fellow who came into my bedroom two weeks ago," she finished for him, her head coming up, her full mouth smiling, and a twinkle in her *grrrr!* eyes.

She was only a head shorter than he, and she stood just a fraction too close for it to be called neighborly.

He was semi-speechless. He stumbled over a word for a few seconds, realized what it was, and used it to start a sentence. "That's right. I—I was wondering if we might not go out for something to eat, and a show perhaps..."

He left it hanging on a questioning note. He knew he was good-looking and had personality.

He also knew that for the first time in his life he couldn't use either of them. He had lost all charm of power of *savoir faire*. He was a bumpkin.

Kingery stared at her dumbly.

"Why, that sounds lovely," she said brightly, taking his arm.

He moved arm in arm with her toward the front door of Pomeroy's. He didn't hear one of the twenty-nine "Good night, Mr. Kingery!"'s thrown his way by sharp-eyed salesgirls.

He didn't know when he hit the street.

And he certainly didn't know he was getting into a cab with Jeanie Belamonte!

The evening had been heavenly. Literally heavenly. He was certain he was walking on pink and turquoise clouds, with Angel First Class Jeanie Belamonte beside him.

The dinner was nectar and ambrosia under glass. The show was *Paradise Regained*. The night club was thrust up through the night sky, leaving them perched beside a softly-glowing star-cluster that whirled and banked as they danced.

He vaguely remembered holding Jeanie close to him, the firm, tight points of her breasts pressed against him, his arms about her, his hand in the small of her back. He even recalled vividly the instant they danced out onto the terrace, over the twinkling and vibrating city, and Jeanie murmured something low and throaty, and turned her face up to his. He remembered as though in a blast of lightning-bright memory, the sight of her beautiful face, the cry of her half-closed, hungry bedroom eyes, and the

sweet, sweet taste of her lips on his, the searching of her hot tongue-tip, the ecstasy of her body
grinding into his own.

Then it all faded into a kaleidoscopic opium-
dream, and he was in the cab, sprinting for his
apartment.

She had turned to him, her thigh pressing
against his own in fierce demand, her hand
guiding his over the thin fabric of her skirt, over
her fiery flesh.

He had leaned closer and smelled the sweet-
ness, the sweet incense of her breath, the sweet
winds rising from her body, and his kisses had
merged, melting, interflowing: one long, sighing
promise.

Her back had arched and she had strained
against him. He hadn't even known when his
hand left the furry feel of her sweater and invad-
ed the domain of her breasts.

They were firm yet yielding, and he touched
them, feeling the electricity of her flowing
through his own body, urging him on.

This was a night even the Gods would have
envied.

Then they were out of the cab and in the eleva-
tor and at his apartment door and in the room,
and he held her even tighter, feeling her trying
to get closer, closer.

He lifted her—she was light as a pillow—and
carried her through the living room, into the
darkness of the bedroom.

Gently he laid her down on the bed. The
moonlight streamed through onto the floor in
broken banners, casting a pale light on the soft
flesh of her revealed legs and knees. Her eyes

were closed, and her breathing was ragged. Her tongue moved over her lips in crying abandon.

He slid his cupped hands out from under her, prepared to lie down beside her...

She sat up abruptly, terror on her face, and clouted him squarely across the jaw. She followed it by a slashing right under the eye, and he went over a chair, landing in a disorderly heap on the floor.

By the time he had regained his feet, feeling the burning across his face, she was out of the room.

Distantly, he heard the front door slam.

He sat back down. It wasn't worth getting off the floor.

All night.

Don was late getting to work at the store the next morning. His head ached with a dull throbbing, and he was so confused, he had taken an hour off to see an old friend—a psychiatrist. He had also applied a beefsteak to the eye.

None of it had done any good. Not the psychiatrist, not the aspirins, not the walking in the cold morning air, and the painful blue cheeks to prove it, not even the ridiculous beefsteak for the swelling. None of it. He still didn't know what the green hell had happened.

One moment she had been a clawing wildcat of a woman, anxious for love—the next she had treated him as though he had propositioned her mother, while he had been undergoing emolument TLC for bubonic plague. It didn't figure.

He hurried to the store, and as he passed before the ComfeeSnooze window he saw Jeanie

leap from the bed, legs flashing, and begin ges-
turing wildly at him. She wanted to talk to him.
She had obviously been waiting some time for
him to show up.

"Uh-uh, lady," he said, making the words big
enough so that she could read his lips through the
store window. He didn't want any more of that. He
fingered his battered eye and glared at her.

Don continued into the store, the problem
getting deeper and deeper, his head throbbing
harder and harder, his libido screaming louder
and louder. What was with this kid?

It wasn't till lunch time, as he was leaving
Pomeroy's, that Jeanie came running from the
dressing rooms, and took his hand. "Don! I've
got to talk to you! I've got to explain."

He looked at her strangely, afraid at any moment that vicious fist would arc up and flatten
him again.

Warily, "Okay, Jeanie. Come on, I'll buy you
lunch."

Over a martini, steaks working on the charcoal grill, he looked at the troubled face, the
worried—yet still appetizing—turquoise eyes
of Jeanie Belamonte.

"What was that all about?" he asked without
preamble.

She seemed hesitant to speak. It took a vis-
ible effort to get the words out. A deep breath
preceded each sentence, and he had a hard
time keeping his eyes off her sweater's round-
ing-out, and eyes fastened with P.C. stickum to
her lips.

"It's because of my job," she answered, mis-
erably.

"What? What's that got to do with it?" he asked.

"I've been 'bedwarming' as you'd call it, for almost six years now. It's all I do now. They book me steady into these kind of things at the model agency. They say I'm the best for this kind of work."

Don could readily agree with her, but kept silent. They had sold four times as many Com-feeSnooze mattresses since Jeanie had been in the window.

But this was getting confusing—embarrass-ingly confusing—more damned confusing than before—hideously more confusing every sec-ond—and he was afraid if he spoke, the whole logic that seemed to be building would evapo-rate. He *wanted* an explanation: it was now ap-parent to him he had to have Jeanie Belamonte at any cost. Even broken noses, blackened eyes, crushed jawbones and concussions.

"I started sleeping all day," she explained carefully, "and after a few months I found I had to stay awake all night. Now I *can't* sleep nights.

"I walk in the park, I iron clothes, I read, I do everything but sleep. It's gotten so that now— I'm—I'm—afraid I—I—" She slurred to a halt, her face screwed up in worry.

She couldn't find the proper words.

"You mean—?" he bumbled, in approved soap opera fashion.

"Yes," she answered hopelessly, "I've got a phobia against beds. I can't lie down in them."

The rest of his lunch was a thing of stunned silence. The steak grew cold and finally he took

her back to her ComfeeSnooze, under the nev-
er-faltering glare of the DayLights. A fog had
closed down over his mind.

This was hideous.

This was frightening.

This was horrible.

This was frustrating!

Jeanie Belamonte had slept so long in store
windows, it was the *only* place she could sleep
now. She wanted to make love, but it was totally
impossible for her. The moment she touched
back to bed, she went pathologically mattress-
buggo and came up swinging.

Don Kingery asked for sick leave that afternoon. He had to have time to think.

He went home and emptied a bottle of Old
Smuggler into himself. Still his thoughts ran in
one—and he admitted it!—track.

How to bed Jeanie Belamonte.

Standing up in a hammock? Ridiculous! He
chided himself. Nailed to the ceiling? Impossible! Empty all the furniture out of the apartment and manage on the floor? Insulting!

In two hours his head felt like the Graf Zeppe-
lin, and he was no nearer a solution. He paced
the floor, kicking viciously at the legs of the sofa,
as though that implement had done him wrong.

"Worthless bastard!" he cursed it.

How was he ever going to walk up and down
in Pomeroy's, under the glare of the DayLights,
between the counters, knowing Jeanie was lying in that window, her heart beating for him,
and he…worthlessly helpless to go to her.

It was a dilemma.

Three hours later, as he stood before the window of his apartment, watching the daylight fade down behind the jagged outline of the city's roofs and antennas, the answer came to him.

He got back to Pomeroy's just as the 5:30 bells were ringing throughout the store. Sales-girls were tallying their money, cloths were be-ing thrown over the counters. The store was emptying rapidly, guards at the doors checking the packages as straggling customers and hur-rying salespeople left. It was Saturday night, and many left as couples.

Don felt the heat of his search mounting in his cheeks. Now that he had a solution—now that it was clear to him—he couldn't wait over the weekend. He had to find her, had to see her that night.

He was sure the vision of those bedroom eyes in his dreams would drive him berserk before Monday morning.

Then he saw her. She was hurrying past a spe-cial sale counter piled high with enema tubes and hot water bottles.

Her face had changed subtly since he had talked with her at the restaurant. The smooth, unlined beauty of her sensuous face was now wrinkled by lines of worry. Her hands were tightly gripping her handbag, the knuckles strained and white.

"Jeanie! Jeanie!" he cried out, across the length of the store.

She turned, saw him, and started walking faster, the slim beauty of her legs flashingly ny-loned as she made for the door. Don elbowed aside customers and sales-people, blind to everyone but Jeanie. "Jeanie! Wait for me! I want to talk to you!"

She was out the door, and he had a momentary tussle with the door guard before he could shoulder past. Then he was on the street, his head swiveling this way and that. Which direction had she gone?

Then he saw her, a few feet to the right. He ran toward her, and a moment later had her by the elbow. His breath was drawing hoarsely, but he got the words out, "Look, Jeanie, I understand. Don't feel bad. I don't mind. Honestly!"

She stared up at him, her eyes beginning to glaze with forming tears. He watched, his heart sinking in him.

"Don't cry, Jeanie. Look—why don't we go out to dinner. Make a night of it!"

It took some tall talking, right there on the sidewalk, with the heat of her next to him, and the staring crowds listening to every word as they passed.

Finally she agreed, and they were off to dinner.

The evening was as marvelous as their first. Somehow, even with the shadow of Jeanie's phobia between them, they found enjoyment in each other's company, and Don sank deeper and deeper into his desire for her.

It was going to be rugged from here on out, with luck the deciding factor—but the stakes were too high to back out now.

After the show—Don had made certain it was a boring melodrama—he took her to a night club where the show was exceptionally miserable.

When they got into the cab, Don whispered an address to the driver, and climbed in beside Jean.

"Clever show wasn't it?" she smiled bravely, in the cab, throttling away from the club.

"Rotten," he disagreed, "and you know it." He smiled at her. She looked tired. After the sleep-inducing show and the boring night club acts, she was really bushed. *Perfect!*

The cab turned down Main Street and kept to the right as the cabbie searched for numbers in the semi-darkness left by the street light glare. Jeanie looked out the window, a frown darkening her even features. She was tired, but still alert. "This isn't the way to my home." Then annoyance and anger flooded her voice. "You aren't taking me to your apartment again, are you, Don? I thought we'd talked this out, and you understood."

"Good God, *no*, we aren't going to my apartment!" he assured her, moving closer. Her face smoothed out again, and a smile broke through.

"I—I'm sorry, Don," she said, patting his arm absently.

"Oh, that's all right, Jeanie, that's all right," he smiled back at her. To himself he thought, *That's just peachy-keen, Jeanie, just peachy-keen.*

Five minutes later they pulled up and the cabbie said, "This is the address you gave me, Mister. That'll be a dollar and sixty-five cents." There was bewilderment in his voice.

"Just right," Don grinned, handing him a five dollar bill. "Keep it," he added, opening the door and helping Jeanie out.

As the cab pulled away, Jeanie looked up at

the totally dark and monstrous shadow before them.

"But this is Pomeroy's," she said, with confusion.

"Right-O!" said Don, leading her to the door.

He pulled out his key chain and opened the door. Leading her inside, he locked the door behind them.

"But—but—what?" Jeanie tried to fathom this thing. It was four in the morning. What were they doing here?

"This is after working hours!" Jeanie protested, trying to make a joke, in place of understanding.

"Oh no it isn't!" Don replied, smiling cryptically.

They moved toward the front window.

At 4:15 A.M. the DayLights shone brightly in the front window of Pomeroy's Department Store. In the window featuring the Comfee-Snooze display.

It was a lucky thing no one was out late in those wee hours. Otherwise they might have seen the most revolutionary window display ever conceived.

Both Ends Of The Candle

FRANKLY, I WAS BEAT to the socks.

When Dorothy Candle opened the front door of her house, standing there with that wispy bit of fluff all ready to be ripped off, all ready to have herself tossed between the sheets—I knew I'd had it! Three months of dating Dot Candle and her daughter Valerie—without either one knowing I was romping in the hay with the other—had worn me to a fine edge of nervous hysteria.

"Are you going to stand out there all afternoon?" she asked, waving a slim arm toward the dim interior of the house. I shuffled in, like a sleepwalker.

"I'm glad you could come over today," she said, after we'd both retired to the living room sofa. "I wasn't sure you were coming when I called you."

"Mmm," I mmmed. She'd called me at the fraternity house, and threatened me with throwing herself off the University Administration Building if I didn't tool over double-quick! Now, it seemed, she didn't even remember her threats.

"You look tired," Dot observed, stretching her arms above her head till the thin, wispy *peignoir* lifted clear of her upper thighs. I took slow notice.

Tired? Why the hell *shouldn't* I be tired? Almost every day, for three months, no sooner had I left Dot Candle off with a kiss in front of the telephone company—where she worked night shift—than

I'd had to drive crosstown to Stalling's Department Store to pick up her daughter Val.

No sooner did I climb out of the feathers with one (who was no slouch, let me observe!), than I'd climb in with the other! Tired? You aren't just masticating rice patties, brother!

"I bought this sleep outfit special for you," Dot smiled showing her white, even teeth. She stood up, on tiptoe in her pink mules, and showed the thing off. She needn't have bothered. I could see right through it.

"Nice," I said, lackadaisically. I felt as though all the energy had been drained out of me by square needles inserted in my brain-pan.

This is the last time, so help me God, I thought. I'll tell her today I'm calling it off between us.

Then, as I saw that look come into Dot Candle's grey eyes, I added, *Later I'll tell her. Later.*

Dorothy leaned over, taking my hand, placing it over the wispy, silky material covering her breasts. "I'm glad you could come, Wendell," she breathed. "We *do* have fun, *don't* we?"

"Yeah. Fun." I'm afraid I wasn't too frisky, right then, but I'd had to stay up all night to catch up for an exam. This thing with the Candle women was talking quite a bit of time. No wonder my eyes were banked with bloodshot lines. My step was getting faltery, and the coach had warned me my timing was way the hell off. If you think keeping two hardy women satisfied doesn't soak it out of you—try it yourself some time!

I didn't have long to worry about it, because in three seconds flat she was all over me, her lips hungry and searching. I found myself rising to her advances, even though I knew I'd be as limp as last week's mashed potatoes afterwards.

"Wait a minute, honey," she gasped, drawing away. "I'll call you in a second." She got off me, and moved away, saying, "I know your football coach wouldn't approve, but mix yourself something from the bar. I'll be ready in a minute." She made a Burley-queen switch with her full hips, swirling the *peignoir*, licked her lips, and made a small animal noise.

Despite myself, I growled, "Rufff!" and she stuck out her tongue at me. She moved into the bedroom, wiggling like a Mixmaster.

I walked slowly and carefully to the bar. I'd found I had acquired a weave in my walk. I opened the bar and found the vodka. "A drink will steady me," I told myself aloud. "Any orange juice around?" I yelled.

Her voice sifted out of the bathroom. "Ice box, naturally."

I got the orange juice, mixed it with the vodka, and settled back down on the sofa with my Screwdriver. For the thousandth time since it had begun, I rolled this whole whacky situation through my weary mind.

I'd met Dorothy Candle three days before I met her gorgeous daughter Valerie. In my third year of college—without actually trying—I'd become a legend on campus. They called me "Minute Man" Asimov. The man with the split-second sex-drive.

It had been one of those completely screwball quirks of fate that brought Dot into my range.

I'd called New York, long distance, one morning. "Dad," I said mournfully, "we've been slapped with an order to buy five new lab books for biology. It looks like it's going to come to twenty-five dollars. I hate to ask you for it, Dad…what with my allowance all used up and everything…but *you* know how it is…"

I'd gotten the promise of twenty-five (which had taken care of those abysmal blackjack debts to the brothers in my fraternity)—and a little bonus. The bonus was the long distance operator on my end, who had called me back fifteen minutes after I'd hung up.

"I'm off-duty," she'd said.

"Oh?" I'd answered, not quite getting the pitch. For all I knew she was a real pig, but her voice had been deep and throaty, like warm butter melting over warm butter. It made *me* feel warm and melty.

"I liked the sound of your voice," she'd said. "I was lonely, and thought we might go out—have a drink."

I'd taken her up on it, and that had been the start. We had gone to her house in the early afternoon, and the warm circle of her arms had enfolded me for the first time.

I'd been seeing Dot Candle steadily—almost every day—ever since. In the afternoons, while Val was at classes and the department store.

I'd met Val three days later than her mother. I'd spotted her in the stands and made the pitch. Her mother hadn't told me her last name—even though we'd gotten very well acquainted—so I was amazed when I went to pick up Val for our first date, and found it was the same house I'd been visiting during the afternoons.

That night I'd found out "like mother, like daughter" was true, all too true.

The madness of the whole thing appealed to me. So, under wild pretenses that they musn't reveal the name of the fellow they were seeing to anyone, especially not their family, I'd kept one from learning the truth about the other.

When I was through romping in the hay with Mommy, I'd drive her downtown in my beat-up Chevy; kiss *her* at the door of the phone company; and go crosstown to pick up her equally lovely daughter; kiss her at the door of the store, and drive back home for a romp in the hay, à la offspring.

It had been Paradise Regained the first month or so. Then it had slowly become the pace that clobbers! I was beat all the time, inefficient in my studies, worthless on the gridiron, hopeless at everything. I looked like the "during" in the "before and after" posters.

I'd promised myself I was going to call this thing off, bid these hot-blooded dolls fond adieu, and go back to sleep for three weeks, but every time they called, I came running. It was a real experience to shack up with a Candle girl!

As though my thought had been a signal, I heard the oozing oleo of Dot's voice from the bedroom. "Ready, Wendell, honey."

I put down what was left of the Screwdriver, and expanded my manly chest for the ordeal at hand. Even though I was bushed to the ground, the thought of her lying there made me hot right through my skin.

The ordeal at hand. That was *just* the phrase for it, too!

Dorothy Candle was stretched out on the bed.

She was a well-preserved thirty-six. Not that you *have* to be preserved at thirty-six, but I've seen plenty of women who looked like empty sacks of alfalfa, at thirty-six.

Dot Candle was no empty sack. Her sack was well-filled. I just stood there in the bedroom doorway for a second…looking.

My eyeballs had a life of their own. They started at the feet and worked up toward the head of the bed. Long, trim legs that were beautifully molded and tapering in their nylon sheaths—just the way I liked her, with her hose still on! Thighs that were firm and round, the blood beating just beneath the surface of the pale skin; hips that swelled enticingly. The eyes paused only momentarily in annoyance at the tiniest bulge at the tummy.

The stomach *did* bulge a bit, but only charmingly enough to make the eyes go looking elsewhere up the frame to make it unimportant. They moved up, past the high, upthrust and inviting breasts, past the white, round throat—and stopped on the face, surrounded by a cloud of auburn hair spread out across the pillow.

Dot was a beautiful woman. Face unlined, full sensuous lips, hot eyes telling me there was a C.O.D. parcel waiting for my taking.

I stripped quickly, and sat on the edge of the bed. Despite myself, my breath was coming in gasps, and my hands were palm-moist and shaking. She came into my arms smoothly—like a well-oiled machine.

She brought her face up, and my lips found hers. It was almost peculiar the way I kissed Dot Candle. As though our lips were magnetized, and they *had* to meet.

She slid her eyes shut, and her body moved against mine.

I didn't realize my hands were moving on her body, till I felt her shift slightly, and I wasn't caressing the thin wispiness of the *peignoir* any more. I was touching the warm, moving flesh of her breast.

Suddenly I buried my face in the warm softness of her breasts, felt the rigid nipples harden under my lips. Her fingers were caught in my hair, pulling, and she was moaning in my ear, low: "Now! Now! What're you waiting for? What? Come on!"

Dorothy Candle's husband had peeled off into a six-foot trench three years after they'd been married, and what with Val to take care of, she'd been making do with what was handy ever since. She'd told me a dozen times I was the only one who could keep up with her.

I took a swan dive, and swam the length of her body. "Nice, nice, nice, nice…" she kept moaning all through it, tossing, and fighting, biting my ear.

At times like that, I was glad I'd had classes in sex hygiene.

I didn't waste much time.

Afterward, I lay there panting, and swearing to myself: *Never again! So help me God, never again!*

This was exactly what I'd told myself I *didn't* want to happen any more.

"That was fine, Wendell," she murmured in my ear, playing with the ripples of my stomach muscles. "You're the greatest. When will I see you again? Tomorrow?"

I slammed my eyes shut, and a little moan escaped between my clenched teeth. I was tuckered out a-plenty. Every bone in my body cried out for sleep. I knew I had two more classes that day, and a week's worth of studying to catch up on before I'd even be back where I should have been. Not to mention Valerie—and *her* insatiable nature.

"Maybe," I groaned weakly. This thing that had seemed so fantastically appealing—dating a mother and a daughter without one knowing of the other—was now a nightmare.

Somehow I got dressed, though I ached in every joint, and drove Dot down to the telephone building. I sweated all the way—*a cappella*.

I gave her the usual tender kiss at the door and drove off, half-asleep. I knew I had to pick up Val at Stalling's in another hour. I got to quivering so badly I thought I'd pile up on a telephone pole.

If I thought the tremor would run down the wire and cold-cock Dot, I might have done it. But I knew it wouldn't, so I did the next best thing. I stopped off at Terry's Bar & Grill and had a quick one.

In fact, I had three quick ones. No sense taking chances. Then I piled back into the Chevy and went over to pick up Dorothy's daughter, Valerie.

She came out the side door a few minutes before the rest of the girls. Even if she hadn't, I would have spotted her. As tired as I was, the sight of those trim ankles, the tossing bob of her carroty hair…and *those breasts!* I felt my dormant pulse speed up from 33-1/3 to 45 to 78 rpm.

Those breasts!

Fantastic!

They were even higher than her mother's, and they were at least a 39—but carried beautifully. They pointed right up. In fact, they were the kind of breasts that made a guy look over his shoulder to see where and what they were pointing at!

The rest of her matched. She was just over five feet six, with all the weight carried in the bust and rump, just the way I liked them. *Zoftig!* But not sloppy; Good Lord, no!

She hip-switched up to the car and leaned in my window. "Don't I know you from someplace, Big Boy?" She smiled.

I usually had a wisecrack for her, but that had been three months before I'd gotten sent through a wringer.

"Mumpf," I wheezed, my head flopping onto the window ledge.

"You don't look so well, Wendell," she said, concerned. "You sick?"

I nodded. "Uh-huh. Come on, get in."

She slid in next to me, her thigh brushing my leg, and it felt like someone had stuck a live wire into me. "*I* know what's the matter with you!" she cried. "And I know what you need to fix it up. Come on, let's go right up to the house!"

I almost groaned and slid under the steering wheel, but she didn't seem to notice.

"I've got something for *youuuuu.*" She drew the word out suggestively, straightening back her shoulders, making her breasts push out against the fluffy cashmere of her sweater. "Let's go."

I could have fainted, right then, but somehow I got the car started and drove back to the house.

Back to heaven's bed that had been the scene of so many heroic bouts between the Candles and me. I was groaning inside. *Never again!* I swore to myself. *Never, never, never, never again.*

So it was back to the house. This time with the daughter, who had her mother beat by a few decimal places. I was beginning to feel like a yo-yo with a pair of everlasting, never-wearing-down, amazingly Amazonian strings. My eyeballs felt watered-down, my legs were buckling from the knees.

That had been the roughest three months of my life—and today wasn't making it any easier.

At the house, while Valerie was busy turning out all the lights but one dim one casting a faint glow, I made myself another quick Screwdriver.

She drew the Venetian blinds, put on Ravel's *Bolero*, and changed in an instant from a reserved, bobby-soxed college co-ed, to a raging tigress.

First she ripped the clothes off me. "Off! Off!" she kept chortling, stripping me down.

"Take it easy with that sweater, will ya!" I yelled, as she yanked it off over my head. "It's got my football letter on it!"

It was a ritual with her—this stripping me down—and I'd learned the hard way not to frustrate this peculiarity. Once she had me bone-naked, she started doing things.

The *Bolero* was just getting loud enough to hear, and she began moving. She'd take a short step toward me, and stop, moving her body slowly, running her hands up her body till they cupped her breasts—those magnificent breasts.

She'd take another step, and turn partially away from me. Then she'd run her smooth, slim fingers down to the hem of her skirt, and rub it up her legs, letting the full expanse of white thigh and marvelous leg show itself. Slow slow slow it would come up, and she'd let the fingertips rest lightly on the firm white skin of her thighs for a second. Then the skirt would come down. Cutting off the sights, just like that.

It always made me gasp.

I was petrified. I could feel my pulses pounding in my temples, my body beginning to sweat. So soon after a woman as hot and demanding as Dot, I was being stirred to animal heat by her daughter.

The music was getting wilder, and she started getting the same way. Her hands came up, and pulled the full bob of her red hair up, till it spilled in a rich cloud over her face. Then her hands slid sinuously down her body, the fingers hooked, till they contacted the bottom of her sweater.

A few writhes and pulls, and she had the sweater off, and the black lace of her bra only one-third concealed the mounds of rose-pink loveliness they contained. "Ch…Ch…Ch…" I found my lips chattering, my eyes wide and burning.

She *shhhed* me to silence with a finger at her full wet lips.

I should mention that I *shhh* easily.

In a moment the bra was off. And here's the beauty of her: the breasts stayed where they were. They didn't spread into a pool of fat and drop to quiver around her belly-button. They were firm and round and tip-tilted—still pointing toward the juncture of wall and ceiling.

It took forever for the skirt to unzip and fall in a tweed circle at her feet. The panties matched the bra.

They didn't conceal a helluva lot, either.

Damn this family! I thought.

The music swelled to a crescendo, and the panties started rolling. Down and down she rolled them, till they were a thin bandeau around her hips.

My body was aching for her. I saw my arms extended in front of me, but so help me I couldn't feel them move!

As the record whirled to a beating finish, she had the pants off, and the dark, matted triangle between the lustrous white of her thighs was revealed. Then she was in my arms, writhing, screaming, scratching at my back with ten little daggers that left ten red furrows, pleading for the same unchained thing her mother had pleaded for!

I never *could* refuse a woman...

The next week went the same way. The daylight hours were spent in mortal combat with Dorothy and her hungry limbs. The darkling hours were tossed away in gay madness with Valerie and her fantastic body.

I was so exhausted, I wanted to snore during my classes. My "deeply concerned" professors warned me I was going to flunk my ass into limbo. The coach wanted to put me on carrot juice. I went from 180 to 155 in no time. I was stopped on campus and asked why my eyeballs were hanging down onto my cheeks. I couldn't answer.

Finally, I decided to stay away from them both—for good.

It worked fine for a few days. I was even beginning to feel a little healthier.

I'd gone without seeing either one for almost a week, when Dot called.

I was sleeping (I had been doing a *lot* of that lately) on a couch in the living room of the fraternity house, when a pledge came over and wakened me. "Woman named Candle on the phone for you, Wendell," he said.

"*Which* Candle?" I asked warily.

"Didn't say," he answered.

"Tell her I'm flying the first ship to the Moon and they can't locate me." I started to lie back down.

"She says something about being preg..." he began, but I was off and running before he'd gotten the last syllable out.

"Hello?" I quavered, into the mouthpiece.

"Hello, Wendell, honey," I heard Dot's melting butter tones. "I haven't seen you all week. Where've you been?"

I lied some, and begged some, and swore some, but she threatened to go to the Dean unless I drove out there right away.

I finally said okay, and went upstairs to change into something that wouldn't get ruined if it was ripped in a hurry.

Before I had a chance to leave, I got another call.

"Hello, Wen?" said Val's voice—strained.

"Yeah," I tried to tough it out.

"I'm pregnant, Wendell," she sobbed.

I almost fainted. Good God, NO! Not two of

them! No, no, no, no, no, no, no...

I told her I'd see her. She said she was busy right now, but that she'd meet me at her house later that night, after her mother had gone to work. She signed off saying, "I'll have to introduce you to my Mom, Wendell. You'll just *love* her!"

All the way to the Candle home, I made sure my mind was blank. *That ain't hard for you, Wendell boy,* I thought.

I pulled up in front of the house and ran up the walk. I pressed the buzzer, and almost immediately the door opened.

By Valerie.

I wanted to fold into the sidewalk, but she licked her lips and said, "Come on in, Wen, honey."

I must have looked like a somnambulist, because she steered me to a chair, directly facing the sofa.

Dot sat on the sofa.

"B...b...but you two don't know each other! You...you...*can't* know..." I stumbled into incoherent jabbering, drooling and frothing.

"Oh, pish," said Val, waving my objection away with one slim hand. "We've known all along. The only reason we say anything now is that you seem to be drifting away."

"And we can't let *that* happen," Dot added, smiling at Val in a motherly manner. "You're the first fellow we've had around in six years that can keep up with us!"

They both smiled at me charmingly.

I wanted to die.

"I won't do it!" I said emphatically. "We're through!"

"Oh, no we're not," Dot said.

"If you say we're quits, I go to the Dean," she continued. "I'll tell him you compromised my daughter. That'll get you kicked out of the university good and proper."

"And," Val added, smiling sweetly, "*I'll* call your father in New York and tell him you compromised me—*and* my mother, and the chances are that'll get you disinherited. You wouldn't like that, would you?"

They kept right on smiling—damn them!

"How much do you want?" I asked.

"Everything," they said together.

"Ev…ev…ev…?" I couldn't get it out.

"We just want you, doll-face," Dot said. "That's all."

My heart went flippity-flop and settled into my tummy.

"Well, I suppose I could make out a schedule…different days for each of you. How would that be?" It was a last-ditch hope. I knew if I didn't work it that way, I'd be a 97-pound scrawny in another three months.

They laughed at me and came over, kissing me. "That'll be fine," Val said, starting to undress.

"Yes, just dandy," Dot agreed, dropping her quickly-unzipped dress.

They stood in front of me, nude. Waiting. It would have made any man pant with eagerness. Me? It only made me want to faint.

"Well, let's go," I said, starting to get up. I got two steps toward the bedroom, and Dot's voice stopped me.

"Oh!" she said.

I turned around and she had an "Oh, damn it!" look on her face. "There's one thing I forgot," she said.

"Yeah? What's that?" I asked, worried.

"You may have to revise that schedule a bit."

"Why?" I asked.

"My kid sister Cherry is coming to live with us next week. Oh, you'll like her, I'm sure. She's got red hair like both of us…"

A Girl Named Poison

(as by "Jay Solo")

THEY WERE waiting for him when he left the bowling alley. Three of them. And the girl. The one with the breasts pointed heavenward like a pair of land-to-air missiles. She was the one who had flirted with him shamelessly in the cocktail lounge adjacent to the lanes.

They were waiting for him, and he went to her like a tot waddling to it's pablum. She was standing just inside the circle of light thrown by the streetlamp, at the mouth of a service street leading to the rear of the bowling lanes.

He should have been tipped by her brazen attitude. Nobody, but *nobody* comes on that way for free; and Harry had sworn, eight years before, after a particularly unpleasant episode with a seven-dollar and fifty-cent hooker, that he would never pay for it again. But he'd had two beers too many, and she was a helluva looking chick, and when he came out between the neon panels of the bowling alley, and she called to him, he moved toward her without caring, wondering or thinking.

She had a wistful little smile on her lips, and it reminded him of a girl he'd known one summer, who had come to stay with an older sister who worked in the same office where he endlessly sorted invoices. The face was different, but it was the same smile, her smile, and that, more than the lust, or the need or anything about it, made him helpless to his reactions. Her hair was a pale, frosty blond, and though the eyes were shadowed by the night and the angle of streetlight gleam, he remembered them from the cocktail lounge as being Dresden blue.

Tilted onto one hip, she stood waiting for him, and as he moved to her, there seemed no reason to speak; so he took her in his arms, and she suddenly went cold and hard and alien to his need for her.

Before he could pull his head back to fathom what had happened to her warmth, one of the three heavies grabbed him by his hair and pulled him into the alley.

It was dark in there, and for a full half minute he could see nothing but the bombshell-red pain flashes of fists exploding against his mouth, his cheeks, the arched bones over his eyes. It was no fight. The first punch caught him flush on the jaw and sent him toppling skittering bumbling backward into the second heavy, who let out a grunt of air and kicked Harry in the groin. He went down to one knee, holding himself, and the third heavy grabbed him by both ears, double-timed a step and brought up his knee into Harry's mouth. The Roman candles popped sputtered wailed and exploded, and the top of his skull went far away. He tried to rise, but there was blood on his face and on his hands, and he kept slipping, and two of the heavies held him while the third worked him over effortlessly, methodically, ruthlessly.

He was long gone into the half-world of a gray-out when he heard the girl saying, "Okay, that's fine. Leave something moving. Take his wallet and his watch and anything else he hasn't got nailed down."

Then, hands were moving over him, scuttling like crabs, and pulling free of his shirt pocket the white envelope with the two hundred and fifty dollars in it. The money he was going to use to pay the medical bills. And his Helbros watch with the lovely slow sweep second hand. And his key-chain, and his wallet, and all his change, and even his sport jacket, which was ripped from skidding into the brick wall of the alley.

There was a moment of returning consciousness, in which he tried to grab onto them, murmuring bloody nothings between his torn lips. He could see it very clearly, somehow—and in his mind it would permanently burn there—perhaps it was the ghostly glow of the streetlight; the beautiful girl, with her pale blond hair swaying smoothly, took three timid little steps to him, locked her fists together, and swung her arms as though they were a battleax. The piledriver caught him low in the throat and he was paralyzed with a pain that made all the rest seem transitory. His breath stopped in his throat, his mouth swelled to twice its size trying to find air, and a shock of ghastly numbing pain sailed freely down his body. The scream was all in his head; and they let go of his shoulders and biceps, and he fell flat-out, face-forward to the concrete. He rolled slightly, and only that saved his nose from breaking, from sending bone splinters into his brain, from killing him right there.

He rolled and lay there.

And she drew back a foot and kicked him as hard as she could in the rib cage. There was a tiny crackling sound in the still alley as her foot met his flesh, and she whispered just low enough to be heard by the night wind, "Dirty old man!"

Harry faded faded vanished in a swamp of pain and torment, with the thought bubbling in him, as the blood bubbled from his mouth: *Old man? But I'm only twenty-seven…*

It didn't matter. A moot point. His mind, a part of it that was not screaming and clutching itself in anguish, heard them strolling jauntily away; and then his throat started to work again, and he realized he was deeper in pain than he had ever been before, even in Korea, and he slid all the way into unconsciousness.

It was the day before Thanksgiving.

And that is how modern fairy tales begin.

Harry Treet left the hospital three weeks later. He walked with a decided limp of the left leg, and his rib cage was still laced and bound up like a Gibson girl in her corsets. His right eye was covered with a patch, and there was an ugly shaved circle on his head where they had worked on the hole left by the shoe of one of the heavies. All told, one hundred and sixteen stitches in his body, but neat; very neat.

The first thing he did was check with the bartender at the alley. Never saw her before. One thing was certain: she wasn't jailbait. A year or two over the line, but no longer dirty-innocent jailbait. He'd told the police he hadn't seen who had done it, and in a way, he wasn't lying. But he didn't want their help. He was going to find them himself. The three heavies and the frosty blond gamine.

He took to hanging around the neighborhood. It wasn't his style. He had always been a solitary man, even during the hellish days in Korea; and after the hospital it had seemed even more necessary to be alone. All alone. But now he was moved by only one hunger—to find that girl. To do to her what she had done to him; to turn back the evil she had dealt him when he needed love; to restore himself to solitary loneliness by retrieving that moment of exposure, when he had opened himself as he swore he would never do.

She had taken a bit of his need, and turned it against him. Now he was going to find her and make her pay for it. He wasn't certain just how far he would go with her, but he knew she was in trouble. As for the three heavies, they were as good as down the hole.

He thought he saw her one afternoon in a grocery, a little Puerto Rican *bodega*, and he sprinted through traffic as best he could with the game leg; but when he pushed through the doors of the store, he saw at once it was an older woman with grey hair, close enough to her frosty blond to be mistaken from a distance. He turned and left, spending the rest of the day slumped on a park bench, smoking. They had told him not to smoke, but he didn't give a damn.

The urgency to find her had blown itself all out of proportion. He could not understand it in terms of hate. He only knew she was his mission, from now on.

And then, on the Sunday following his mistake, Harry Treet saw the girl. This time, for real. It was her. She was walking toward Prospect Park with a tall, broad-shouldered young man. Harry could not tell, but he seemed to be one of the three heavies. He followed them, at a distance.

The girl did not seem to be involved with the man, because he tried to take her hand at one point, and she shook it off, moving apart from him a few inches. They continued walking toward the Park.

Harry dropped back and hobble-hopped across the street, turning down an alley and coming out on the other side, parallel to them, but one street over. He raced as best he could, with his leg in such crummy shape, till he came to the Park. He slipped across the Avenue, and into the Park, and took up a position midway between the street where they were walking and the street he had come down.

There they were. He watched as they looked both ways to catch the flow of traffic. Then they jumped, almost as one, as native New Yorkers have learned to do, into the whizzing maelstrom of heavy traffic, standing absolutely motionless like hounds on point, as the tons of hurtling metal spun past them, then darting into another clear space, standing, darting and finally gaining the opposite side.

They walked on farther, toward Harry, where he stood concealed behind the thick bole of a tree. He watched, and as they came abreast of him, he could hear her saying, "Candy, I *told* ya, I'm not gonna do it. Andy made me do it the other couple times, and I did it 'cause I'm his deb, but you ain't nothin' to me, and I *will not* do it, so f'get it..."

The young man hauled her to a stop, a few

feet past Harry, who had slid around the bole of the tree to continue watching, but remain concealed. Now Harry felt his jaw muscles tightening as the young man, Candy, dragged the girl back to him. He pulled her up close, wrenching her arm up in its socket till she was on tip-toe.

"Lissen, you dumb little bitch, I don't give a shit how much you don't wanna do it; and I don't give a damn about Andy, neither. He's the Vice-Prez of the club all right, I know that, but I need some bread, too, and the best way t'get it is to hustle some yo-yo the way you'n Andy got it worked out."

"Well, I *won't*, so let go of me! Candy! Let... go...of...me...!" And she kicked him. It was a solid whack against his shin, and he fell back, but still holding onto her. Then she jacked her knee up into his crotch and he let go hurriedly.

She turned and ran.

Right into Harry Troot, who stepped out from behind the tree, cocked back his right, and took her high on the point of the jaw as she raced toward him. The sound of it was like a thick twig cracking over someone's knee, and the girl went down in a tidy flurry of thighs and petticoats.

Candy was just getting to his feet, his face ashen, when Harry took ten quick steps to him and bolo-punched him full in the stomach. Candy, who had been one of the heavies in the alley that night, was concrete in the stomach muscles. He *wooooshed* air and settled into a "U" at the force of the impact, but in a second he was back, and offering his jaw for Harry's left. Harry brought it up from just above the knees, and took him flush along the left side. It skittered up

Candy's face, whanged off his eye-socket ridge, and sent him backward into the grass.

He struggled to get erect, and Harry did a peculiar hop-skip to him, and with his good right leg, kicked Candy as hard as he could, in the throat.

Candy fell back, arms wide as though he were singing an aria from *I Pagliacci*. His eyes rolled up, glazed, and then the eyelids fluttered closed, and he went to the nice land of soft pink-and-white bunny-rabbit dreams.

Harry—breathing raggedly from his taped ribs and the strain of exertion—stumbled back to the girl, and grabbed her by the frosty blond ponytail.

Unceremoniously, he dragged her to her feet. She came back to consciousness in fits and starts, and when she came fully awake, her hair pulling her up tight like a topknot, and saw Harry, and began to cry.

"That would tear my heart out if I hadn't been there when you kicked in my ribs, baby." Her mouth made a small "o" of terror as she realized who Harry was, and she struggled to get away from him. He grabbed her arm and pulled it back up behind her. "Okay, Rapunzel, we're going to go someplace and talk. And then I'm going to decide whether to kill you myself, or turn you over to the fuzz."

The girl tried to break away, and he yanked the arm up more tightly. She subsided, and he said, "Move!" They walked across the Park, and so intent on the beautiful painful girl with him, and the fury of his emotions, had Harry become, that he did not see Candy raise himself jerkily on one elbow, and stare through slowly-clearing eyes as they walked.

Harry did not see Candy try to rise to one side, fall back, try again and this time succeed. Nor did he see Candy dragging himself erect, to steady himself on the tree.

Nor did he suspect Candy was watching them, following them as far as he could with his eyes, and slowly hobbling after them when his eyes could no longer track their passage.

Harry saw none of this, for he was suddenly locked in a tiny world with the blonde girl. Locked in, and possessing no keys.

"My name's Marni," she said, surly and frightened.

They were sitting on orange crates, on the roof of a tenement where Marni had told him she lived. Her story was that she and her older brother shared the apartment.

"Fat chance," Harry snarled. "Which of those three animals that pounded me do you shack-up with?"

Her face grew red, then she snapped, "I'm not lying! You've got cause to be bugged at me, but I'm telling you the truth! My brother Bob and me are the only ones left; Mom and Dad got killed in the Remington Shirt fire two years ago August. It was in all the papers, you must'a read about it."

Harry nodded.

"Well, I wasn't old enough to shift for myself, and Bob has taken care of me ever since."

"He's done a lousy job, if you ask me," Harry said.

"Yeah, well that's what you think!"

"Yeah, *exactly* what I think! If I had a sister who was running around the streets like a tramp, balling with every rumdum and jerk, mugging guys outside of bowling alleys, switchin' her butt through the Park in the middle of the day with bums, I think I'd take a club to her!"

Marni's face grew furious. "A helluva lot *you* know! Listen, wise guy, on this block, in this turf, a girl don't even *breathe* unless she belongs to a club; even a jerk like you outta know that." Then a sadness passed across her fine features, and she started to cry again, softly. "It wasn't like this when Mom and Dad were around. Then Bob and all of us used to go for a Sunday on the Staten Island Ferry, or out to Coney, or take a show at the Paramount. It was real nice; I was a kid then.

"But then Mom and Dad got caught on the tenth floor when the Remington went up, and Bob had to get another job to support the both of us, and I started waiting tables at Ken's, down the block there." She pointed over the side of the building, down into the street, where Harry saw a string of small shops and one-arm joints, one which said KEN'S EATS on the front window.

"Yeah, so?"

"So! So, I had to start walkin' these streets again to get to and from, and one day this buncha bastards stopped me and backed me up against an alley wall and told me they thought I outta belong to the club. They was gonna do it to me right there in the alley—one guy had his hand in my bra and another one had his hand up my skirt—and I was scared out'a my mind.

Then along came Andy, he was the Vice-Prez of the club, and he told 'em to back off me.

"So I kinda liked him, and he asked me if I'd be his girl, his deb, and I said yeah, because it was easier than gettin' raped every time I went out for a loaf'a bread. And I hadda go through initiation—so don't tell me about hard times, buddy—and I was Andy's chick."

Harry felt a tightness in his chest. "You must like this Andy a lot."

Her face changed altogether. The lips drew back and her teeth seemed to become fanged. "I hate him! That filthy bastard. He's made me do things I can't stand, I can't look in a mirror. You, f'rinstance, I'm sorry about that, real sorry. But I had to help them, or they'd have beat me up…or worse."

"You certainly seemed to be enjoying it."

"I wasn't. I even went to the hospital to find out if someone like you had been brought in, I finally found out you'd be okay."

"No one told me."

"I asked them not to. Told them I was an old girlfriend." She grinned shyly at that. Harry smiled back at her.

"Do you still want to kill me?" she asked.

He shook his head. He was beginning to feel like a kid on his first date. After Korea and the hospital, and what they had told him, and then getting beaten up, and *back* into the hospital, not to mention the time spent looking for her, his emotions had gotten all clogged up. But he suddenly realized that he genuinely attracted to her. She was no kid, but there was a charming innocence about her, even after what she had been through, what they had made her do.

"Would you like to come downstairs for a cup of coffee?" she asked him. "I'm sure Bob has gone to his other job now. He works swing shift at night, and in the afternoon goes to a plumbing company to help out."

Harry accepted, and they went down to the apartment. It was a typical Brooklyn railroad flat, a straight-thru, with the kitchen at the front. They sat around the table, and she made him a cup of instant coffee, which he hated, but somehow it tasted just fine, there with her.

They talked for a while longer, and then she said, "I'm sorry about what happened. I had to do it, but what happened *inside* the alley, I wasn't putting that on. I really liked the way you looked, and you seemed to be such a nice guy."

"Maybe under different circumstances," Harry said gently, "it might have been different."

She leaned across to smile at him, and almost without his knowing it, she had looped her arms around his neck and her mouth was tight to his. He knew she was no kid, but when her full mouth opened and the molten heat of her breath mingled with his, he forgot the scene in the bowling alley completely. He stood up, pulling her erect with him, and she flowed to him, and their bodies were tight together. She was more buoyantly built than he had thought, and he was barely aware of the fact that he was trying grind his body into hers.

Then she was murmuring, "W-we could go into th-the bedroom...uh...if you w-w-want to."

So they walked close in each other's arms,

into the bedroom, and she pulled the shades, and he undressed her very slowly, very carefully, very lovingly, and her naked body was clean and sweet and perfect, as he had known it would be. Clean and white as she lay there quietly, waiting while he stripped out of his T-shirt and his slacks and came to her. They lay there quietly, side by side, for a long moment, then she gave a tiny moan of anxiety, as though she thought he was never, never coming to her, and her arms came up. He bent across her, then, and kissed her thoughtfully, longingly, in the hollow of her throat, her eyes, her breasts, and in an instant they were fused as a flame of passion leaped down between them, welding them together.

He did not know how long they lay there, straining, parrying, discovering each other, but he knew that even if Korea and the hospital had happened, it was not all in vain. If it had to be, at least he had this moment of pure, nameless, golden luxury.

He was murmuring fine things in her ears, and she was responding with little nibbling kisses, when they heard the banging at the front door.

Marni leaped up and pulled her clothes on quickly. "Bob!" she said. Adding nervously, "But—but *he* shouldn't be back yet!"

Harry dressed as quickly as his pained rib cage would allow, and he followed her into the hall and down its length to the kitchen. The noise was incredible. Whoever was out there, whanging on that door, it wasn't her brother. Then a voice came through the door, howling with frenzy, and another behind it, and a third. "Open the goddam door, open it you little scummy bitch, open that door!"

"Andy!" Marni hissed, and her eyes spread wide with terror.

"Get back there," Harry commanded her, and shoved her back behind him, into the hall. At that moment the force of three bodies hit the door, and it bowed as though it were made of rubber.

It was a typical Brooklyn Flat, and the kitchen was very small. From the door to the opposite wall, across the room, was no more than twelve feet; and outside, the hall itself was narrow. *If they hit that door hard enough*, Harry thought frantically, *and I open it, they ought to go straight across and hit the wall. That might give me time …*

He stared across the room at the table, the refrigerator, the stove, the window that gaped directly across from the door…trying to estimate what obstructions they would carom off, till he could get at them.

Harry stepped behind the door, and as he heard the three bodies gathering force to strike again, he slipped the bolt. The door hung open, and the three heavies hit it full steam. The door rebounded off the inner wall, and Harry jumped back just in time to avoid being brained. The three bodies came hurtling through, and one of them went right on across the narrow kitchen, into the window, smashed it, and disappeared. All in one fluid movement. They could hear his scream all the way to the pavement four floors below. The thunk! as he struck concrete was sickening.

The other two—one of them was Candy from the park, still carrying himself with pain from the beating Harry had given him—caught themselves. Candy on the side of the refrigerator, and the remaining gang member—obviously Marni's Andy—across the table.

Andy came erect, and stared at them with open hatred in his ruthless young face. "So you was *ballin'* with him! I can tell. So you was doin' it with him, you filthy slut! I'm gonna take him, an' then I'm gonna cut you up real slow and nice, in little ribbons, and dump you in every garbage bucket on this block!" And as he said it, his hand snaked down into his boot, and came up with a knife.

He pressed the stud on the side, and six inches of honed German steel leaped into view with a snick!

He dropped into a crouch, and Candy moved in high behind him. Harry squared off with a *little fist*: primary Tai Kwan Do stance.

Marni screamed, high and keening.

Andy lurched forward, Harry slipped aside, and before Andy could bring the blade back into strike position, he was inside his guard, his flattened wedge of a left hand came screaming out in a wide, flat arc, and took Andy straight across the upper lip. Andy shrieked in a woman's tone, and the knife went clattering under the stove, and he fell backward with blood crimsoning his face. The nose was broken, and the skull formation damaged. He flailed back into Candy, who tried to get out of the way as blood spattered the linoleum. Harry was on them in an instant. Two quick chops, and a savate kick, and Candy went down for good.

"Call the police, Marni," Harry gasped, leaning against the wall. "Tell 'em come get them. I think the one downstairs is gone; and if they don't hurry, Andy'll book, too."

She went to call the police, and came back to him.

They waited in silence, his hand in hers, and when it was finally over, when they took the two gang kids away, Harry was alone with her.

"I—I'd like to be your g—girl now, Harry," she said, very young and very embarrassed.

"I think I'd like that just fine," Harry said. But there was a knot in his chest, even as he said it. The knot was more than emotion. It was something growing in there, something he picked up in Korea, something the doctors at the hospital said would kill him soon. Not in a week, or a year, perhaps, but soon enough.

He had been drinking and wasting his time till it caught up with him, until that night when she had flirted with him and his life—what was left of it—had been given over to finding her. And somehow, it was all for the best. Because now, for however long he had—and he would not tell her it was coming—he had something to live for, someone to cling to.

And for the first time he didn't mind that he was going to die. He had never really cared, and that was why he had taken the chances he had, but now it mattered, now he wanted to stay around, to see how golden he and Marni could get.

And it was a fairy tale.

They would live happily ever after.

But this was a modern fairy tale.

So they would not live happily ever after— forever.

Not forever.

No one ever does.

CHRONOLOGY OF BOOKS BY HARLAN ELLISON 1958-2012

NOVELS:

WEB OF THE CITY [1958]

THE SOUND OF A SCYTHE [1960] [2011]

SPIDER KISS [1961]

SHORT NOVELS:

DOOMSMAN [1967]

ALL THE LIES THAT ARE MY LIFE [1980]

RUN FOR THE STARS [1991]

MEFISTO IN ONYX [1993]

SHORT STORY COLLECTIONS:

THE DEADLY STREETS [1958]

SEX GANG (as by "Paul Merchant") [1959]

A TOUCH OF INFINITY [1960]

CHILDREN OF THE STREETS [1961]

GENTLEMAN JUNKIE and Other Stories of the Hung-Up Generation [1961]

ELLISON WONDERLAND [1962]

PAINGOD and Other Delusions [1965]

I HAVE NO MOUTH & I MUST SCREAM [1967]

FROM THE LAND OF FEAR [1967]

LOVE AIN'T NOTHING BUT SEX MISSPELLED [1968]

THE BEAST THAT SHOUTED LOVE AT THE HEART OF THE WORLD [1969]

OVER THE EDGE [1970]

ALL THE SOUNDS OF FEAR
(British publication only) [1973]

DE HELDEN VAN DE HIGHWAY
(Dutch publication only) [1973]

APPROACHING OBLIVION [1974]

THE TIME OF THE EYE (British publication only) [1974]

DEATHBIRD STORIES [1975]

NO DOORS, NO WINDOWS [1975]

HOE KAN IK SCHREEUWEN ZONDER MOND
(Dutch publication only) [1977]

STRANGE WINE [1978/2004]

SHATTERDAY [1980]

STALKING THE NIGHTMARE [1982]

ANGRY CANDY [1988]

ENSAMVÄRK (Swedish publication only) [1992]

JOKES WITHOUT PUNCHLINES [1995]

ВСЕ ЗВУКИ СТРАХА (ALL FEARFUL SOUNDS)
(Unauthorized Russian publication only) [1997]

THE WORLDS OF HARLAN ELLISON (Authorized
Russian publication only) [1997]

SLIPPAGE [1997]

*KOLETIS, KES KUULUTAS ARMASTUST MAAILMA
SÜDAMES* (Estonian publication only) [1999]

LA MACHINE AUX YEUX BLEUS (French publication
only) [2001]

TROUBLEMAKERS [2001]

PTAK SMIERCI (THE BEST OF HARLAN ELLISON)
(Polish publication only) [2003]

DEATHBIRD STORIES (Expanded edition) [2011]

PULLING A TRAIN [2012]

GETTING IN THE WIND [2012]

OMNIBUS VOLUMES:

FANTASIES OF HARLAN ELLISON [1979]

DREAMS WITH SHARP TEETH [1991]

COLLABORATIONS:

PARTNERS IN WONDER: Collaborations with
14 Other Wild Talents [1971]

THE STARLOST: PHOENIX WITHOUT ASHES
(With Edward Bryant) [1975]

MIND FIELDS: 33 STORIES INSPIRED BY
THE ART OF JACEK YERKA [1994]

I HAVE NO MOUTH, AND I MUST SCREAM:
The Interactive CD-Rom (Co-Designed with
David Mullich and David Sears) [1995]

"REPENT, HARLIQUIN!" SAID THE TICKTOCKMAN
(Rendered paintings by Rick Berry) [1997]

2000X (Host and Creative Consultant of National Public
Radio episode series) [2000-2001]

THE DISCARDED (with Josh Olson) [2011]

GRAPHIC NOVELS:

DEMON WITH A GLASS HAND (adaptation with
Marshall Rogers) [1986]

NIGHT AND THE ENEMY (adaptation with Ken Steacy)
[1987]

VIC AND BLOOD: THE CHRONICLES OF A BOY AND
HIS DOG (adaptation with Richard Corben) [1989]

HARLAN ELLISON'S DREAM CORRIDOR,
Volume One [1996]

VIC AND BLOOD: THE CONTINUING ADVENTURES
OF A BOY AND HIS DOG (adaptation with
Richard Corben) [2003]

HARLAN ELLISON'S DREAM CORRIDOR,
Volume Two [2007]

PHOENIX WITHOUT ASHES (art by Alan Robinson
and John K. Snyder III) [2010/2011]

NON-FICTION & ESSAYS:

MEMOS FROM PURGATORY [1961]

THE GLASS TEAT: *Essays of Opinion on Television* [1970]

THE OTHER GLASS TEAT: *Further Essays of Opinion
on Television* [1975]

THE BOOK OF ELLISON (edited by Andrew Porter)
[1978]

SLEEPLESS NIGHTS IN THE PROCRUSTEAN BED
(edited by Marty Clark) [1984]

AN EDGE IN MY VOICE [1985]

HARLAN ELLISON'S WATCHING [1989]

THE HARLAN ELLISON HORNBOOK [1990]

BUGF#CK! The Useless Wit & Wisdom of Harlan Ellison
(edited by Arnie Fenner) [2011]

SCREENPLAYS & SUCHLIKE:

THE ILLUSTRATED HARLAN ELLISON (edited by
Byron Preiss) [1978]

HARLAN ELLISON'S MOVIE [1990]

I, ROBOT: THE ILLUSTRATED SCREENPLAY (based
on Isaac Asimov's story-cycle) [1994]

THE CITY ON THE EDGE OF FOREVER [1996]

RETROSPECTIVES:

ALONE AGAINST TOMORROW: A 10-year Survey [1971]

THE ESSENTIAL ELLISON: *A 35-year Retrospective*
(edited by Terry Dowling, with Richard Delap &
Gil Lamont) [1987]

THE ESSENTIAL ELLISON: *A 50-year Retrospective*
(edited by Terry Dowling) [2001]

UNREPENTANT: *A Celebration of the Writing of Harlan
Ellison* (edited by Robert T. Garcia) [2010]

AS EDITOR:

DANGEROUS VISIONS [1967]

NIGHTSHADE & DAMNATIONS: *The Finest Stories
of Gerald Kersh* [1968]

AGAIN, DANGEROUS VISIONS [1972]

MEDEA: HARLAN'S WORLD [1985]

DANGEROUS VISIONS (the 35th anniversary edition)
[2002]

JACQUES FUTRELLE'S "THE THINKING MACHINE"
STORIES [2003]

THE HARLAN DISCOVERY SERIES:

STORMTRACK by James Sutherland [1975]

AUTUMN ANGELS by Arthur Byron Cover [1975]

THE LIGHT AT THE END OF THE UNIVERSE by Terry Carr [1976]

ISLANDS by Marta Randall [1976]

INVOLUTION OCEAN by Bruce Sterling [1978]

THE WHITE WOLF SERIES:

EDGEWORKS 1: OVER THE EDGE & AN EDGE IN MY VOICE [1996]

EDGEWORKS 2: SPIDER KISS & STALKING THE NIGHTMARE [1996]

EDGEWORKS 3: THE HARLAN ELLISON HORNBOOK & HARLAN ELLISON'S MOVIE [1997]

EDGEWORKS 4: LOVE AIN'T NOTHING BUT SEX MISSPELLED & THE BEAST THAT SHOUTED LOVE AT THE HEART OF THE WORLD [1997]

EDGEWORKS ABBEY OFFERINGS:
(IN ASSOCIATION WITH PUBLISHING 180):

BRAIN MOVIES: THE ORIGINAL TELEPLAYS OF HARLAN ELLISON (Volume One) [2011]

BRAIN MOVIES: THE ORIGINAL TELEPLAYS OF HARLAN ELLISON (Volume Two) [2011]

HARLAN 101: ENCOUNTERING ELLISON [2011]

HARLAN 101: THE SOUND OF A SCYTHE AND 3 CLASSIC NOVELLAS [2011]

MOTION PICTURE (DOCUMENTARY):

DREAMS WITH SHARP TEETH (A Film About Harlan Ellison produced and directed by Erik Nelson) [2009]

AUDIO COLLECTIONS READ BY THE AUTHOR:

ON THE ROAD WITH HARLAN ELLISON (Volume One) [1983/2001]

THE VOICE FROM THE EDGE: I HAVE NO MOUTH, AND I MUST SCREAM (Volume One) [2002]

THE VOICE FROM THE EDGE: MIDNIGHT IN THE SUNKEN CATHEDRAL (Volume Two) [2001]

ON THE ROAD WITH HARLAN ELLISON (Volume Two) [2004]

RUN FOR THE STARS [2005]

ON THE ROAD WITH HARLAN ELLISON (Volume Three) [2007]

THE VOICE FROM THE EDGE: PRETTY MAGGIE MONEYEYES (Volume Three) [2009]

ON THE ROAD WITH HARLAN ELLISON (Volume Four) [2010]

ON THE ROAD WITH HARLAN ELLISON: HIS LAST BIG CON (Volume Five) [2011]

ON THE ROAD WITH HARLAN ELLISON: THE GRAND MASTER COLLECTION (Volume Six) [2011]

WATCH FOR THE SECOND HALF OF THIS TRAIN: "GETTING IN THE WIND"

OTHER KICKS BOOKS
YOU WILL ENJOY

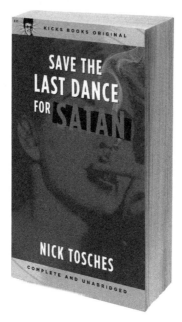

KB1 *Sweets and Other Stories* by Andre Williams
KB2 *This Planet is Doomed* by Sun Ra
KB3 *Save The Last Dance For Satan* by Nick Tosches
KB4 *Pulling A Train* by Harlan Ellison
KB5 *Tall Cool One* by Kim Fowley
KB6 *Getting in the Wind* by Harlan Ellison

WILLIAMS · SUN RA · TOSCHES · ELLISON · FOWLEY

KICKS BOOKS
PO BOX 646 COOPER STATION,
NEW YORK NY 10276
www.kicksbooks.com